Something Great and Beautiful

Something Great

· AND ·

Beautiful

A Novel of Love, Wall Street, and Focaccia

ENRICO PELLEGRINI

OTHER PRESS • NEW YORK

Production editor: Yvonne E. Cárdenas
Text designer: Jennifer Daddio / Bookmark Design & Media Inc.
This book was set in Cochin by Alpha Design & Composition
of Pittsfield, NH

1 3 5 7 9 10 8 6 4 2

Library of Congress Cataloging-in-Publication Data

Names: Pellegrini, Enrico, 1971– author.
Title: Something great and beautiful : a novel of love, Wall Street,
and focaccia / Enrico Pellegrini.
Description: New York : Other Press, [2018]
Identifiers: LCCN 2018000923 (print) | LCCN 2018005184 (ebook) |
ISBN 9781590519745 (ebook) | ISBN 9781590519738 (paperback)
Subjects: | BISAC: FICTION / Satire.
Classification: LCC PQ4876.E355 (ebook) |
LCC PQ4876.E355 S66 2018 (print) | DDC 853/.914—dc23
LC record available at https://lccn.loc.gov/2018000923

Of his bones are coral made.
Those are pearls that were his eyes.
Nothing of him that doth fade,
But doth suffer a sea-change
Into something rich and strange.

—WILLIAM SHAKESPEARE,
THE TEMPEST, ACT 1, SCENE 2

The Maestro, or
How to Die in the Arms
of a Beautiful Woman

CHLOÉ VERDI

What does it mean to climb inside a white tiger's cage? Challenge or carelessness?

Or to kidnap a Labrador on the Italian Riviera in your orange bikini? Ridiculous or lucrative?

And how did I get from there to Wall Street? Initially I'd hoped it was my brains, then I settled for my ass, but at the end of the day wasn't it merely because I was born in Genoa and speak Italian?

Already, these questions were assaulting my mind, my lungs, my heart, like busy bees.

And how does it feel when you want to hear his voice, and you stare at the phone, and the damn thing doesn't ring?

Or when the phone rings and it's your boss, and even though your law degree is just as good as his, he wants you to . . . organize a soccer tournament for the firm's associates?

Or it's your boss and now he wants you to . . .

what? . . . work on an IPO on the stock exchange, yes one of the biggest deals of the year, Ms. Verdi.

Or when the phone rings again and it's the police?

And the prosecutor wants to know every little detail about your life? And he wants to turn over every stone in your past? Where did you meet him, why in India, what were you doing there, what was he doing there? And how did you get here?

The bailiff summoned, "All rise!" and everyone stood up as Federal Justice Henrietta Pontia Pilgrims entered the courtroom. I had been subpoenaed to testify and I was the key witness and the seven largest U.S. banks had collapsed and the love of my life was facing 137 years in jail.

CHLOÉ VERDI

May 4, 2009, New York

India, Ms. Verdi?" asked the prosecutor for the Southern District Court of the State of New York, looking at his notes and then pausing to stare at my lime-colored skirt. In one glance he made me feel that it was both too bright and too short. "How did you first meet the defendant Rosso Fiorentino in India?"

ROSSO FIORENTINO

I was dropped off at the edge of a village an hour outside of Calcutta and found myself standing inside a backyard in the middle of nowhere. It was a hot and humid afternoon and there was only one cloud in the sky; for some reason it reminded me of a blank check.

Everyone was preparing to celebrate the Meindith, the first day of a Hindu wedding. When I asked, a weak, bony hand pointed across the yard to the Maestro, possibly the greatest writer alive—the man I had applied to work for and whom I'd traveled so far to meet. I would soon discover that my job to serve him would only last one single night.

"What can I do for you?" I asked immediately upon our introduction, in order to make a good impression. "What would you like, Maestro?"

"A gin and tonic," he said.

I hurried to the far corner of the yard, where someone from the Maestro's hotel had set up the "bar": two bottles of gin standing on a wooden bench next to a pile of melting ice.

"Is it Hendrick's?" the Maestro asked when I delivered him the drink.

"Gordon's," I said.

"It's Gordon's?"

"Yes."

"Do they have piña colada instead?"

"No."

"The hotel didn't bring my piña colada?"

It was hard to tell his age because of his tanned cheeks and his playful, yellow, seersucker jacket. He did not look like one of those Westerners who goes to India in search of something spiritual. A thick coat of gel made his white hair positively shine in the daylight.

"How old are you, Rosso?" he asked, tucking in his shirt.

"Twenty-four," I said.

He studied my face for a moment.

"And how old were you when you acquired this badge of valor?" he said, pressing his thumb against the scar on my chin.

"I prefer not to talk about it."

"That's fine. But do tell me. What made you respond to the ad?" Companion for renowned writer in India, it had read. Travel and living expenses covered. Otherwise unpaid. "You can speak plainly," he said. "Nobody else responded."

"I want to be a writer," I said.

"Okay," said the Maestro. "What's plan B?"

The shadows grew longer and the white moon slowly brightened. Women in orange saris, toes sticking out of their sandals, lay large banana leaves across the floor where the guests would eat. The village houses had no electricity and the evening sky began to glow over their darkening rooftops. My big cloud was breaking up into many white scraps, as if the check had bounced.

"Would you like to try a dosa, Maestro?" Sachin asked, handing the old man a completely burned pancake.

Sachin was the Maestro's driver and tour guide, who had picked me up at the airport. With his small stature and voluminous hair, he looked like a miniature of someone, an eighties rock star, perhaps. He was five feet one inch of pure ambition. What he lacked in height he more than made up for in confidence, but he had a tic: whenever he was tense, he looked up as if something was about to crash on his head.

"I would like another gin and tonic," the Maestro said, rearranging his jacket. The last button of his shirt had come open and I noticed a blue plastic bag under it.

"How are you feeling?" I asked.

"Empty," the Maestro said smiling. "That beautiful sense of emptiness I felt as a kid."

And all of a sudden, as the celebration took shape around us, the Maestro began to speak, as if he had to tell us his whole life. Emptiness, emptiness, he spoke a great deal of how he considered emptiness a virtue, almost a privilege—he remembered how his first experiences had tumbled nicely inside of him—an empty, clean self—with a distinct echo: his first kiss at sixteen with Leslie on the Brighton Beach promenade; his first reading of Hemingway's *The Sun Also Rises*; writing his own first novel.

Women in bright saris were starting to dance, but Sachin and I both gave the Maestro all of our attention.

"I chose not to get married," he said with untamed pride, "and not to have children, because I wanted to be the best novelist of my generation."

He believed that in order to write well, you needed to be perpetually infatuated, ever on that dizzying edge of falling in love, and because, at some point, such limerence fades away, as a writer you could never be in a single relationship for too long. But sometime in his mid-thirties, he told us, despite his bachelorhood, the world began to fade on him, to lose its echo, its bright edges, its power to inspire. The more memories, prizes, romantic adventures piled up in his stomach, the more that beautiful sense of emptiness turned into numbness.

For the past ten years, he told Sachin and me, he'd felt like an old mansion sagging with too much furniture. "It's not that I was indifferent; I was full."

After that point, he'd only published a novel every ten years or so; his inability to feel a shiver, to laugh from his belly and not from his nose, to really cry, and most importantly to fall in love (although he tried to have sex regularly, he specified) made it impossible for him to write.

"Now, though, after the surgery in June, something has changed," he said, groping the little blue bag inside his shirt. It felt as if deep in his guts, someone in his very body, "the movers," he called them, had begun carting stuff away.

He then spoke to us about death, although I'm not sure I understood everything. I guess this was his bottom line: we spend so much of our lives thinking about it that it almost becomes like a real job. "We'd better make the most of it," he said. "This dying." It seemed he had something particular in mind, though I had no idea what. Perhaps, I thought, looking from him to Sachin and back again, the night will tell.

At eight o'clock in the evening the women began to sing as they danced in the backyard, careful not to step onto the banana leaves where the banquet would take place. They moved lightly in a circle, in observance of local rituals, and sang a song mocking the future groom. There was no instrumental music—only their clear, breathy voices. The women were all dressed with great care, but some had open wounds on their faces—some skin disease, no doubt—and flies would land four or five at a time on those whose flesh was still raw.

"Can you hand me my notebook?" said the Maestro, suddenly smiling. I followed his gaze. A red knee-length skirt, unsuited for the occasion, was crossing the backyard. The young woman stood out in a thousand ways, including her casual T-shirt, her fair skin, and her briefcase, which she carried with the uncertainty of a freshly minted newsroom intern. Long, black curls fell on her shoulders like a stream of lava.

"You're going to write, Maestro?" Sachin asked excited. Then he looked at me. "Are you deaf or what, Rosso? Come on, give him his notebook. You're as slow as a glacier in the Himalayas."

The Maestro stood up and headed to the pile of melting ice we called the bar. I followed silently. The dark-haired girl was now sitting on the bench, wearing a press badge. CHLOÉ VERDI, it read. She crossed her legs in a professional way, only to uncross them a second later as she bent over to retrieve a sheet of paper that had fallen onto the ground.

"No thanks," Chloé said as the Maestro pushed a drink toward her.

"It's a gin and tonic."

"I don't drink."

The Maestro tried to make eye contact but she looked straight in front of her. He gave a friendly snort while holding the bag inside his shirt; he always seemed afraid it might open.

"Are you waiting for your boyfriend?" he asked.

"If you're here to pick up girls," she said, "then yes."

Around nine o'clock the banquet began. The backyard looked out onto the open countryside and just beyond that, absurdly, a zoo. Our table was set with Sheffield silverware and a linen tablecloth from our hotel, while the other guests sat on the floor, each eating from a large green banana leaf. There was one empty seat at our table. The father of the bride continued to smile in our direction, no doubt because the governor of Calcutta had paid for the entire wedding and given him three thousand rupees to invite the Maestro and his following. The father of the bride looked young, twenty-four or so, he could have been my age.

Finally he rose and came to our table. He too had a large wound on his cheek. A little snarl of flies settled upon it as he stopped walking and stood before us, though he didn't seem to mind. Chloé Verdi, the dark-haired journalist, was standing just behind him, holding her briefcase.

"This mahili is asking for the Maestro," he said. "She says she is a journalist."

"With *Repubblica*," said Chloé.

"Please have a seat." The Maestro stood up politely and pointed to the empty place next to him, and with a smile said, "You must have decided I look like your boyfriend after all?"

"I'm sorry, I didn't mean to be rude," said Chloé, her cheeks flushed. "I usually recognize the people I see in newspapers... But your face—it's different in the photographs, more..."

"Younger?" asked the Maestro.

She sat between Sachin and the Maestro. As her fingers cut the naan, the warm buttery Indian bread, her eyes still didn't seem to know where to go. Their color was of an uncertain green with a bit of yellow, like two beautiful drops of petroleum.

"How long have you been writing for *Repubblica*?" asked the Maestro.

"Not very long. I'm finishing school in Genoa."

"But how old are you?" asked Sachin.

"Twenty-one," said Chloé.

"They've sent an intern to interview the Maestro?" Sachin said horrified.

"I understand the Maestro never gives interviews."

"But he just told us his life story," I said.

"Maybe so, but word is he doesn't like reporters," she apologized, tucking back her hair. "So the paper couldn't send a correspondent out here just to carry his luggage, if that ended up being the case. So they sent me."

"And that's why we're sending Sachin off to bed," said the Maestro. "So that he doesn't ask silly questions." He did, too. Despite his temper tantrum, Sachin was driven back to the hotel where we stayed.

At the end of the banquet, the digestifs were served; we were presented with a variety of almond teas, anise seeds, and laurel leaves, to be chewed until they became saliva and washed away the evening's spices. My throat was on fire from the white pepper. Finally, we were invited to set off into the open countryside to meet the bride.

We walked in a line, singing an Indian folk song. Now I no longer felt the spices in my mouth, just a pleasant energy. Farther ahead the moonlight glittered on the metal cages of the zoo. In the grass I could glimpse Chloé's shadow; then she was strolling along next to me. For a moment, her eyes dropped down to study the scar on my chin.

"Where are you from?" she asked.

"New York," I said.

"I love New York!"

I had just scored a thousand points.

"Everybody loves New York, except those who actually live there."

"After I graduate in May," she continued, "I'd like to go to law school and work in the U.S. Do you still live in New York?"

"No, I'm at Genoa University, myself."

Her smile faded. "And why would you be there?"

So as quickly as I'd won them I had lost my thousand points, but it didn't really matter. I was taking a holiday from serious relationships.

"I'm working on a novel," I said.

"Like the Maestro," Chloé said, smiling again.

It was odd to bump into her only now. Four years in the same city in Italy, same university, the same department even. Where have I been? I wondered. The grass below my feet seemed longer, damper.

"Funny that we meet here for the first time," she said, as if she were reading my thoughts. "Do you ever go to class?"

I didn't have to answer, for we'd just reached the edge of the field where Premi, the bride, was sitting under a tall banyan tree next to her mother. She had the red powder bindi painted on her forehead and her big dark eyes were sleepy. She was awkwardly tugging the bottom of her white sari between her legs as if she had to pee.

"Damn, how old is the bride?" I asked.

"Almost seven," said Chloé, turning to the Maestro as if he was the one who had asked the question. "Dowry age. It could be a good title for your book."

Kamu, the eight-year-old groom, was sitting under a different tree, because he was not supposed to see the bride. He had a serious look and his small head proudly wore the brown heavy turban of the Punjabi.

"Why would it be a good title?" asked the Maestro.

"In India dowry goes up with age, so families try to marry off their daughters as soon as possible, sometimes even before they're born," the journalist explained. "The older they are the more you have to pay. Among the poor people of course. I mean, isn't that why we're here? Because you're going to write about this?"

"No," said the Maestro as he walked along.

The folk songs grew more distant, and the wet grass grew taller around us. The Maestro continued on as though he intended to reach the border of India, leaving the wedding party utterly behind, and we followed him. Why were we there then? To hide the sweat that trickled to his lip he pinched his nose. Now and then a flock of ducks awakened by our footsteps lifted up into the night sky.

We arrived at the zoo, which was dark, but the gate was open and there was no security guard at the entrance. We followed the Maestro inside. The gravel crackled under our feet.

We passed the metal cages, some of them empty, others filled with restless monkeys. I was reminded of the Maestro's first book, in which a group of strangers run away together. When we reached the central cage, we found a marvelous white tiger stretched out across the ground. The moonlight was so clear we could see the dust on the tiger's fur.

"Can you imagine," the Maestro said, "that on New Year's Eve two drunken Australian students tried to put a garland of flowers around her neck? The next day the zookeeper found only the garland."

We stood still, astonished by the tiger's beauty and size.

"Shall we climb over?" he asked.

"I don't think that's a good idea," I said.

"You have to take risks, Rosso, if you want to be a writer," the Maestro said. He pointed at the scar on my chin. "You have to fuck up much more than that." He turned to Chloé. "Are you afraid too?"

The white tiger was sleeping. Her head was enormous.

"C'mon, Chloé, you look like a tough kid," said the Maestro, brushing his thumb along the inside of the journalist's arm. It was then that I first noticed she too had a scar. A whole map of them, in fact, along her arm. "Unlike Rosso, here, every insult to your flesh has emboldened your spirit, am I right?"

Chloé climbed up with one hand. With the other she tried to keep her red skirt down, pressing her fingers against it, in order not to flash her white underwear more than necessary. Once she reached the top, she jumped inside the cage with one graceful leap. Behind her, the Maestro was climbing slowly, panting, clutching the bag under his shirt. He would give back all the prizes he had won in his life if only it would stay closed.

In a moment, there they were, both inside the cage and only a few steps away from the animal.

"I wanted to be next to a white tiger," said the Maestro.

The tiger's coat appeared almost yellow. Her mouth revealed two dry gums.

"It's sedated," Chloé said. "I hope."

The Maestro uncapped a bottle of Drakkar Noir he kept in his yellow seersucker jacket pocket and took in a deep breath of the cologne. An absurd and desperate habit of his, I would learn, one I imagined quickened his spirits, returned him from the dullness—the fullness—of his present moment to that electrifying emptiness of his youth.

"It's harmless now," Chloé whispered, staring at the elegant beast.

"Like me," the Maestro said.

"Oh, I don't think so!" Despite the danger, Chloé couldn't help laughing. Then she whispered again. "I think it's best if we head back now. Tomorrow the wedding starts early."

When we arrived at the Maestro's hotel, which overlooked the village, it was one o'clock in the morning. Sachin, Chloé, and I were all also staying there. The servants were replacing the torches in the garden. The flames' intermittent light made the sprinklers glitter. As we reached our floor, two guards in pearls uniforms stood with crossed lances in front of each room. It was painful to imagine that just a ten-minute drive separated those elegant guards from the flies landing on the raw flesh of the women's cheeks.

The Maestro's male nurse was waiting in the anteroom of his own quarters.

"Don't look, Rosso," said the Maestro.

The nurse, lithe and efficient, began to treat the wound over the Maestro's abdomen right away. The surgery in June had opened a hole in his colon; the blue plastic bag was attached to it. The nurse emptied the excrement from the bag.

"Why the tiger's cage?" I asked. "What was that all about?"

The old man shrugged.

The windows were open. Outside, the sprinklers ticked. The moon was so red and clear you could count its craters.

"I think I like her," said the Maestro. "Don't you think she's cute?"

Leaves and branches from the garden outside cast large shadows on the wallpaper above the Maestro's bed.

"What, Chloé's not your type?" asked the Maestro, observing my silence. "Can I go for her?"

"She's all yours."

It was a deal. We shook hands.

"Please don't look!" the Maestro repeated.

After arranging the blue plastic bag over his artificial anus, the nurse gave me a nod to accompany him to the door. I followed him.

"I must speak with his next of kin," he said just inside the doorway. He smiled sadly.

"The Maestro has no kin." I said it simply. It was a fact. He had no one.

The nurse looked me in the eye, then handed me the old man's blanket. It was covered in blood.

It was late, of course, but the Maestro ordered a bottle of Riesling and a lobster, since the moon had just turned full. He thought that lobsters tasted better right after a full moon; they were meatier because they had eaten all night long.

He said that deep inside his stomach, over the last hours, "the movers," as he called them, had been working hard.

Outside, the entire village seemed to be awake. Dozens of young boys and girls stood on the flat rooftops. They steered their colorful kites, careful not to tangle the lines in the sky. A small group broke off and ran after a red monkey that jumped from one gutter to another.

"What can I do for you tonight, Maestro?"

The Maestro pressed the bottle of Drakkar Noir hard against his lips, under his nose, and then fluttered his fingers before him as if he wanted to point to objects beyond the walls of his room: the white tiger; the raw flesh on the women's cheeks; Premi and Kamu; and all of the hunger of the world.

"Do what I couldn't do," he said. "Do something great and beautiful, Rosso."

Without understanding what he meant, his words sounded like a lifetime mission.

"No, what can I do for you now?" I said. "I don't want you to be scared."

"I'm not scared," the Maestro said smiling, although he was very scared. "It's been the job of a lifetime to learn how to die. We just need to wait now and see how it is."

After meticulously picking off the pink meat from the large lobster, which was so sweet, he washed his hands and placed a palmful of gel in his hair. He then went out to the hotel's corridor across the hall.

"Are you still hoping for the interview?" asked the Maestro, trying to push away the two guards standing in front of Chloé's door. He knocked energetically as he called out the question.

After a few moments, the door opened and the guards stepped aside. Chloé came out into the hall, rubbing her eyes. She was barefoot, wearing a short cotton nightshirt with a pattern of yellow dragonflies. Suddenly the door next to hers opened wide.

"You're giving your first-ever interview to a twenty-one-year-old intern?" screamed Sachin in his pajamas in a state of shock.

"She climbed inside a tiger's cage," said the Maestro. "You go back to sleep. Otherwise I will authorize the use of force."

As the guard pointed the lance at Sachin, he quickly got back inside his room. Chloé and I followed the Maestro down the hall and then to the car park.

"Who's driving?" I asked, since Sachin, the driver, was left behind.

"You are," said the Maestro.

After my car accident I didn't like to drive anymore, especially a 1985 Fiat Ritmo Abarth with electric features I couldn't comprehend. I turned on the engine and concentrated. I drove with the windows down, the way the Maestro liked it. I drove so carefully that a guy on a bicycle and then two cows passed us. The road was pitch dark. Waves of light green dust and the scent of jasmine came in through the open windows. In the back seat, Chloé was still in her nightshirt, which she held down with both hands so that it wouldn't blow into the wind. Her long black hair went everywhere. I concentrated on the road.

When we arrived at the observatory, a cloud covered the moon. The same Maharaja who had built the palace we stayed in had built this observatory to count the stars. The instruments were made of gray stone, some dark and others aglow. A tree with large white flowers gave off a steady perfume. I parked by the entrance.

"Goodbye, Rosso," said the Maestro.

"Goodbye?"

"Remember, do something great and beautiful," he said, taking the car keys out of the dashboard and closing the windows. A clunky hum followed. He was locking me inside.

"And what would that be?" I asked. "What is that something great and beautiful?"

"That you have to figure out yourself."

The Maestro and Chloé walked inside the ancient observatory, I could see them facing one another. It was funny, they sat in a concave hemisphere designed to measure the spring equinox. As Chloé would later describe it, he spoke slowly so that she could take down everything.

He told her of the summer of 1945, when he bought penicillin for his grandfather who had pneumonia—it was the first penicillin to arrive from America and it was sold in ice blocks on the black market in Genoa.

He spoke of reading Alberto Moravia's *Agostino* for the first time, and how many oysters he ate the night he was awarded the Premio Cervara, Italy's Book Award. He told of how beautiful his first kisses were, and how damn beautiful that first kiss at sixteen was, with that Leslie, again, on Brighton Beach's promenade. For a while he had struggled because of her Indochina politics, but then she surrendered to his Russian politics.

"Indochina politics...?" Chloé asked, confused.

"Yes," the Maestro said, "she gave up the North to defend the South."

Chloé raised her hands to her breasts, guarding them, then dropped them on her nightshirt. "Like this? And what are Russian politics?" she asked laughing.

"Farewell to Moscow."

Chloé listened, and continued to ask questions, and was so taken she no longer took notes. She pulled back her hair as she did when she went out on a date. Almost without noticing, her lips had landed onto his.

The Maestro gazed at the slow, black caress of her hair against her cheeks and at her eyes green like petroleum, and tried to summon his strength to say something, to use that old smile he had used for sixty years and which always worked, maybe to slip inside her nightshirt—who knew?

But now his vision—and her gorgeous jaw line— were blurring.

"You're shaking!" Chloé said.

With a final effort, the Maestro managed to block her hand from rescuing him, from unbuttoning his shirt and reaching to his little blue bag that had become part of him. He lay down on the cold ground next to her. Even if he had waited with fear and torment for this moment, even if it had been the job of a lifetime to get here, it now seemed simple. He almost felt stupid for having wasted so much time, so much energy, thinking about his death. He felt stupid and happy that it was so simple. This was how he wanted it, not on a bed, not in a clinic, but on a stone built to calculate the spring equinox and in the arms of a beautiful woman.

· JOB 2 ·

Sachin, or the Art of Street Selling

CHLOÉ VERDI

May 4, 2009, New York

Good to know about India and where some funny, deranged thoughts of his might have come from...Can you now tell us about Rosso Fiorentino's past in Italy and about street selling?" asked the prosecutor. There was a snicker in the courtroom. "Street selling, Ms. Verdi? Just what exactly was his business education?"

ROSSO FIORENTINO

July 2, 2006, Portofino, Italy

When my mother pulled open the blinds back in Italy, the noon sun invaded my bedroom and rested on the copy of our family crest, which was hanging on the wall in front of my bed. My eyes slowly adjusted to the sun. I liked looking at that crest—five burgundy stripes glinting against a background of gold—but it didn't mean much anymore. After twelve underperforming generations, my father had long since sold our title, a common practice among Italian nobility in need of money, so that he could countinue to be a painter and play bridge. According to my mother, I was the one who was supposed to turn things around.

"What's all this smell of cologne?" she asked, waving her hand in front of her nose. "What are you still doing in bed at this hour? Is your big career plan to become a perfumer?"

I hid under the pillow the small bottle of Drakkar Noir cologne I had purchased at the duty-free in New

Delhi upon my return from India. I didn't inherit any genius or inspiration from the Maestro, but it's good, the Drakkar. He was on to something. I had tried to inhale it the way he did, but had sprayed too much in my room.

"What the hell are you doing with your life?"

"I don't know," I said.

"'I don't know, I don't know,'...you used to have a lot more to say."

That may have been true. I'd lived in New York until I was ten years old. My father, the artist, wanted to explore the New York art scene. When he lost his inspiration, we moved back to Italy and I enrolled in high school in Turin. On my nineteenth birthday, I woke up in a hospital, after a three-week drug-induced coma. I couldn't remember anything except that a minute ago—a split second ago, it seemed—I'd been driving and that my girlfriend, my sweetheart, my love, Marinella, was beside me. Her body, her breath, her smiles and kisses and fingertips. I had seventeen fractures in my face, a hole in one lung, and my tongue was sliced through.

"Are you going to look for a job today?" she asked.

"Noblemen don't work."

"Today, everybody works, you idiot boy!"

My mother says that I strive to do absolutely nothing. But it's not true that I'm lazy. Whenever I conceive an idea, a voice inside me that is more heart and gut than brain says immediately: Rosso, please. You can't even steer a car.

Before leaving my room, my mother handed me the mail. I opened it. My bank account read unequivocally: balance 611 euros.

At around three o'clock I walked down the hills toward the Piazzetta of Portofino. The lion sun— as they call the sun here between two and four in the afternoon—was out and strong and everything seemed to be motionless, as if somewhere a real lion were wandering around. The air was dry and the palm trees barely moved. Even the maritime pines, with their cheerfully crooked branches, were utterly still.

And then I saw it, the port of the dolphins. Portofino. Something in my blood was alive after all— my heart still skips a beat to this day every time I see those little houses painted orange. Yet those little houses are more expensive than a mansion in London, Dubai, or New York. Nietzsche called this part of Italy "the world's belly button" and poet Ezra Pound played his best tennis here. During World War II, the SS commander of the Nazi army was ordered to blow everything up to stop the U.S. forces. According to the books, he couldn't find the courage and sent the following telegram to Hitler: Portofino is too beautiful.

My own task there, that late morning, was economic, to try and find a job, or at least to make some money. I had taken with me my copy of our family crest, the only thing I owned which could be worth something.

There were two street peddlers already at work in the Piazzetta: Sachin, our former driver/tour guide, and a Lebanese sunglasses dealer named Joe. Sachin was kicking a cardboard box that lay on the dock like a soccer ball. The cargo boat had just come in from Madras.

"Look what the fuck they sent me!" he yelled.

Sachin had a degree in electronic engineering, but in Calcutta he could only find a job as a driver/tour guide. Thus he had decided to come to Italy with me and become a street vendor.

"I was expecting Ray-Bans or trendy, summery wraparounds," he said, pointing to a box. "And look what they sent me!"

I looked inside. A pile of green military trousers lay neatly folded beneath a layer of cedar mothballs.

"How can I sell Indian army uniforms at the beach?"

"Pretend they're wraparounds."

"As always, you're completely useless, Rosso."

"Or just return them," I said, pointing to the mailer sticking out from the box. "You have the receipt."

"That's not the receipt."

As he kneeled to reach for the sealed envelope, the light in his eyes changed. He suddenly turned calm, like a follower inside a Hindu temple the moment before the goddess Kali appears.

"Will you?" he asked, handing the sealed envelope to me.

I tore it open and began reading: "'Dear Mr. Sachin Asghar...we enjoyed your charming manuscript, *The Venus with the Singing Nipples*...'" I burst out laughing. "The who with the what?"

Sachin did his thing—held his breath and looked up as if something was about to crash on his head. The sun was hot. The sea was white and flat and luminous.

"'But...,'" I continued reading.

"But?"

"'But unfortunately it doesn't fit our editorial list.'"

Sachin kicked the box again. He knew that sentence by heart.

"The Venus with the Singing Nipples," I said. I'd never heard the like.

I gazed at the glittering sea with a mix of envy, admiration, and despair. For the past five years, I had been trying to write a novel about my car accident, while now the engineer/driver/tour guide/vendor had written a book in a single month. Sachin had gained the ability to write from the Maestro, while I seemed to have absorbed only the peculiar habit of sniffing cologne.

"Where did you get the idea," I asked, "for a book? To write a book?"

"Do you remember when Chloé, the journalist, asked the Maestro why he had never married?" said Sachin. "I decided to write a book about that. About how you find a wife."

The perfect opposite of what I'd absorbed from that night in Calcutta.

"Right," I said. "The journalist. Wasn't she from around here?"

"Chloé, of course. We're seeing her tonight."

"What do you mean?" I asked.

Somehow—again totally unlike me—Sachin recovered immediately from the rejection. He stuck two fingers, his thumb and middle finger, under his tongue and whistled to the other vendor on the promenade, Joe the Lebanese.

"Hey, come here! I'll give you two of these in exchange for three Ray-Bans."

Joe walked over and looked at the merchandise.

"Two uniforms of the Indian army? No thanks, man."

"Army uniforms aren't the most obvious seaside attire," I conceded.

"Sachin is capable of selling almost anything," said Joe. "The only thing he can't sell is his book."

"Shut the fuck up, guys!" whispered Sachin. "Virginia and Ginevra are here. Look."

A long, silent, midnight-blue Maserati had pulled over by the promenade. No other car was ever allowed inside the Piazzetta of Portofino. When the sixteen-year-old twins stepped out of the vehicle, I felt as if my past had just driven into my present. As in a photo from the 1920s, Virginia and Ginevra were dressed in matching sailor suits *alla marinara*, summer-style uniforms with blue stripes on white. They belonged to Italy's richest family and their summer residence was Portofino's most beautiful villa, but to me they were only the younger sisters of my lost Marinella. Especially Virginia resembled her so closely: the delicate white line of her neck, her grace, the coils of hair that spread across her shoulders like snakes of gold. I looked at the horizon. I looked at the stupid uniforms. I did not look at them in the hope they didn't see me.

They walked on the Piazzetta, carefully observed by their nanny's severe eyes peering out at them from the car. Because they belonged to Italy's royalty, they were subject to certain strict rules. During the school year they weren't allowed to go out at night, but in the summer at the seaside, their curfew was eleven. They came all the way to where we stood. My heart was in my throat. Fortunately, around the time of the accident, the press had very few photographs of the eighteen-year-old who was in the car with Marinella. So I was fairly sure people didn't know who I was. With the twins it was different. I had been to their house, I had dated their sister, I had even met them, although they were children and perhaps didn't remember.

"Go ahead, you ask!" Ginevra elbowed Virginia. Thankfully they didn't recognize me.

Virginia stepped forward. She took a deep breath, as if she was about to say something important. She whispered, "Tonight we're going clubbing at the Covo... Do you have some cool wraparounds?"

"Wraparounds are out of fashion this year on the Riviera," said Sachin, lowering his high-pitched voice to a professorial tone.

"And what's in 'fashion' this year... machine guns?" Joe laughed, pointing at the military uniforms.

"So do you have something hot or not?" asked Ginevra impatiently. "We don't want to look like two schoolgirls at the Covo."

My miniature Indian friend proudly picked up one of the uniforms, unfolded it in the air, and launched into some sort of ballet, looking like a cross between a torero and a valet directing traffic in a car park. He concluded his show by throwing the jacket's uniform in the sky. The ranks shone on the brass emblem.

"You're not going to look like schoolgirls in one of these."

"We're not going to a military parade!" said Ginevra, bursting into laughter. "And at the Covo it's hot."

"At the Covo there's a swimming pool." Sachin resumed his professorial tone. "Underneath you only wear your bikini."

"Hard to find something this cool, even at a flea market," Virginia murmured, playing with a roll of bills in her pocket. Then a look of suspicion came over her face as she examined the trousers. "But the pants have a tear!"

"They were torn by dynamite."

"Real dynamite?" asked Virginia, handing him two one-hundred-euro bills.

That was my life. Outlandish. Haunted. Selling whatever you can sell in the most beautiful pocket of the world hoping that lovely teenagers don't recognize you.

The young twins left holding two army uniforms, and Joe patted Sachin on the back and all the bystanders stood up and applauded as if they were at the opera.

Sachin," I said, my voice small. "Do you think you can sell this?"

He and Joe stopped laughing, perhaps because of the sound of my voice, and looked at me.

"What is it?"

"My family crest."

I was following in the footsteps of my father, who had sold our noble title to a banker with aristocratic ambitions. Anyway, I told myself, we had copies of the family crest in every other room of the house.

"To sell something," Sachin said, "we need a good story." He held up the frame and looked at the five burgundy stripes glinting beneath the glass against the background of gold. "Do we have one?"

I told him what I knew. Apparently we descend from an old princely family from the eleventh century. In the year 1010 an unknown soldier, my ancestor, had killed two mercenaries who were raping a woman, and Emperor Otto the First wanted to knight him. "What is your family crest?" asked the emperor. "This," answered the soldier, my ancestor, wiping his five bloodied fingers on his golden shield. And our crest became five burgundy stripes on a background of gold.

"It's a good story," said Sachin. "How much do you want to sell it for?"

"It's a copy," I said. "If we get a couple hundred euro it's a lot."

"I'll get you more than that."

At around three o'clock the first ferryboat of the afternoon arrived and a herd of sleepy tourists started to trot around Portofino. Some sat down at Puni to enjoy the view, some grabbed a gelato at Il Molo, and an elderly couple came toward us when they realized that all the other stores were closed for the siesta. The couple was from Tulsa, Oklahoma. The man, Larry, wore a pair of shorts and a T-shirt with a picture of the Colosseum, and his wife, Liza, was in a flowery Chanel dress with cute knotted shoulder ties. He had the fixed gaze of a tough guy; she looked naive.

"How much are those?" Liza pointed to a pair of fake Prada sunglasses lying on the sheets at Joe's feet. She did not seemed interested in Sachin's military uniforms.

"Eighty-six euros," said Joe.

"And those?"

"The Ray-Bans are sixty-five, but for you I can make it sixty."

Liza touched the pearls on her wrinkled neck and continued to look around, hoping that Joe would lower the price further before she began negotiating. She was not as naive as she seemed to be.

"And what's that?" she asked, pointing to the frame.

"This is a crest from the eleventh century," said Sachin.

The elderly woman looked at the frame closer.

"What are those red stripes?"

"It was the year 1010..." Sachin began to deliver his own rendition of the story I had told him. He more than tripled the number of mercenaries my ancestor had allegedly killed before he got to the punchline. "…and the princely crest became five burgundy stripes on a background of gold."

The woman smiled, mesmerized. "This is quite something, Larry, isn't it?"

"It is," said Larry, who was checking out a passerby in her micro bikini and was paying no attention. To keep up the conversation he added, "How much is it?"

"Oh, this is not for sale."

"What do you mean?" asked Liza, looking at Sachin.

I was confused too.

"My friend Rosso here," said Sachin turning to me, "is the executor of a will and is taking the crest to an appraiser. He has received offers from various collectors and from one museum."

"What the hell are you talking about?" I whispered. I was even more confused.

"Easy, we can appraise it here and now," said Larry smiling.

"Not possible," said the miniature Indian.

There was a moment of silence, as if he had guessed the two words that Larry most detested. "Not possible" was not part of his DNA. He specified that he had started a hardware store in Tulsa, which was now the second largest in Oklahoma.

"Can you provide additional background about your family?" asked Sachin formally.

"Of course I can. Why?" asked Larry, flattered.

"According to the will, the crest may only be sold to 'a noble person,' defined as a person either of aristocratic descent or showing qualities of high moral character, such as courage, generosity, or honor. Do you think you may qualify?"

The copy of the crest was sold for 3,600 euros. The elderly couple rushed back to their hotel in Santa Margherita to gather the rest of the cash in fear that the price would continue to rise. My miniature friend was a hell of a rainmaker. We ended up splitting it 60 percent to Sachin and 40 percent to me on the basis that he had taught me "how to street sell."

The unspoken code among unlicensed street vendors on the Piazzetta of Portofino is the same as it is everywhere: the first one to see the police is sworn to warn the others, so that everything is quickly put away before the police see it. That evening, at around six, the warning came and the air was suddenly filled with mysterious signs.

A Nigerian vendor waved a rug in front of a café, Joe whistled, and all the street peddlers made a pretense of joining the ferry line with the other tourists. Then the police, the coast guard, passed by in their shiny ivory moccasins, fashionably holding their white caps beneath their arms, pretending to ignore what was going on.

"How did you get away with that?" I asked astonished.

"We dress the police head to toe," said Sachin, winking at me. "They love to buy our Ray-Bans at half price."

· JOB 3 ·

The Octopus Gang,

or How to Steal

to Pay for Law School

CHLOÉ VERDI

May 4, 2009, New York City

Were you and Rosso Fiorentino part of a gang back in Italy?" asked the prosecutor. A cold shiver went down my spine. "Why don't you tell the jury about the Octopus Gang, Ms. Verdi?"

ROSSO FIORENTINO

July 4, 2006, Rapallo, Italy

When Sachin and I finally arrived at Pozzetto Beach, it was ten o'clock in the evening. We had walked all the way from Portofino to Rapallo, a resort town nearby. The days were long this time of year, and the sun had just set. There was one red stripe of light left on the horizon. The beach was almost empty except for a group of boys sitting on a rock. They hovered shirtless over a map of the Riviera, planning their target for the evening. The sea was as flat as a lake.

"That's Federico, the painter, our lucky charm," said Sachin, pointing to a young boy with blond curls so neat they seemed to be sculpted in marble. "He paints like Giotto but is deaf like Beethoven."

Sachin had only been in town for a month and already he knew everyone. Trying not to lag, I pointed to a guy who, from the distance, was larger than a cliff. "And that," I said, "is Don Otto."

"I know Don. Twenty-nine-year-old baker and still a virgin. He joined the gang because I fixed his oven. Good to have a big guy like him around."

The engineer/tour guide/street peddler was all over the map.

"He makes the best focaccia in Rapallo," I tried.

"Right, what the fuck else would he do? He never went to school," said Sachin. Then slowly, almost deferentially, he aimed his index finger toward a highly chiseled face covered by a pair of Fila sunglasses. "Franz, on the other hand, next year he's going to the University of Chicago for his master's degree."

"I know who Franz is," I said, recognizing "the master of parties," as we used to call him back then. Franz could make or break a party; he decided who would be invited and who wouldn't. Furthermore, he dated the woman we all wanted: Marinella. Flashes of tuxedos, sherry glasses, tulip-shaped swimming pools, and the rest of my misspent youth assaulted my mind. Franz, like the twins, was a figure from my past I had managed to steer clear of, until now. "And her?" I asked.

A girl in a white-and-blue-striped T-shirt was standing up on a rock giving orders. At regular intervals, she threw a Swiss Army knife in the air and artfully caught it by its handle. The blade danced in the dusk. She held a large, oily slice of focaccia with her other hand. Her green eyes glinted like a lizard's in the fading sun.

"Isn't that the journalist?" I asked. "When did she start playing with knives?"

"Chloé is like a Ferrari. She changes gears fast."

The rest of the gang joined Sachin and me at the water's edge.

"A swim to warm up for the mission!" Chloé announced. She cheerfully removed her striped T-shirt to reveal an orange bikini and took a last bite of focaccia. I imagined her bikini was happy covering her beautiful breasts.

It was the beginning of summer and the water was still cold. We dared each other to outswim each other. As in my party days, Franz took the lead. Don Otto, the baker, slapped at the waves as if they were pans of focaccia, while Federico, the blond fourteen-year-old painter, struggled with two inflatable water wings. I tried to swim calmly. Now and then I saw a white jellyfish floating ominously in the depths. I didn't want to be part of a gang.

When we returned to shore we dried ourselves, feeling the cool evening air on our goose-bumped arms. The last streak of sunlight had vanished, leaving the sky an intense and darkening blue. They went over the plan again.

"The target is Eugene, a six-year-old Labrador,"

said Franz. He always knew precisely the habits of important people. "It belongs to Kiki, the patriarch's third child. His favorite hobby is to burn Eugene's tail. So we're actually doing the dog a favor. Don't think of it as kidnapping a family dog. We're rescuing him."

"For ransom," Chloé muttered.

"Why are we kidnapping a dog?" I asked.

"For Franz and me, to pay for law school in Chicago," Chloé said. "For the rest of us, to pay the rent." I could see then that she, like the twins, didn't recognize me. I was officially a phantom in my own life.

Franz, on the other hand, knew very well who I was, but pretended not to. From his dark eyelashes and never-ending cheekbones, there glowed the light of someone who makes it big in life, a light so strong that even Chloé had to look away and study her nails. Years ago, however, I had managed to steal Marinella away from him. If Franz had been the companion of my misspent youth, and once upon a time the master of parties, now he was on his way to the University of Chicago to become the next big-shot lawyer. He seemed to do everything well.

"Yep, unlike you, he knows how to move on," Sachin whispered in my ear. Then he looked up as if something was about to crash on his head. "You want me to take a medium close-up shot of the dog, Franz?"

"Fuck, Calcutta, this is not a photography course!
Obviously, you have to show the dog's snout and eyes,
otherwise they don't pay us."

"So Franz and I handle the alarm. Don Otto, you
do the garden," said Chloé. "And you..."

Our eyes met. She hesitated, she still didn't
remember.

"Where did we...Are you part of the gang?"

"He's not," Franz said with a grimace. His eyes
shone. "He must be initiated."

"Really?" Chloé asked.

"Really."

Complying with the order, she pulled out her Swiss
Army knife. She moved the blade close to my cheek. I
felt that first pinch on my skin. But then she stopped.

"Wait," she said quietly, holding the blade to my
face. "I remember you." She had her back to the gang,
but I could see as she lowered her gaze to the scar on
my chin.

"He's already been initiated," she said. Our eyes
locked. She retracted the knife and touched my skin,
running her fingers along the groove of the scar. I felt
her fingertips. For some reason, suddenly, everything
came flooding back. Marinella's amber hair and the
party, and the tires sliding, and the car flying into the
air and crashing into a thousand pieces.

"You okay?" asked Chloé. She smiled. "With that
scar you make women fall in love."

I turned away.

"Come on, Rosso, stop playing the prince," Franz laughed, though his voice was laced with coldness. "Even after a swim you still stink of cologne."

We walked toward the target guided by fireworks. That night was the Feste di Luglio, the July festivities, in honor of the Madonna of Monte Allegro. Down there, in Rapallo, the procession was already crossing the narrow streets, the *caruggi*. They seemed even narrower from up here. The crucifixes were held high above the crowd, dangling in the sky, heavy and immense.

The more I walked, the more tense I grew. I dried my hands with my poplin tuxedo-pocket handkerchief, a remnant from my former party life. Before I knew it, we had arrived at the villa.

After climbing the protective wall, we dropped down inside one at a time. Fireworks lit the sea. An intermittent light appeared and disappeared on the villa's facade. As if awakened by the explosion of a firework, the dog came to us from out of the bushes.

"Do I take the picture now?" Sachin whispered.

"Yes, what are you waiting for, Santa?" said Franz.

When the Labrador raised his snout to look at us, my Indian friend snapped. The camera's flash stunned the dog's sad, sleepy eyes.

"What the fuck do I write?" asked Franz. He turned to Sachin while pressing a red marker onto the photo. "Come on, Calcutta, you're the writer!"

"Three hundred euros per ear."

"Not bad, lean and mean."

Federico and I muzzled the Labrador. The animal gently accepted the muzzle, bowing his neck slightly forward to make it easier for us. Maybe because his owner was torturing him, the dog seemed glad to be abducted. He looked at us, panting a bit. A stream of saliva had dried in the salt-and-pepper fur of his snout.

I climbed up the wall, and Federico handed the dog to me. A soft smell came from the bougainvilleas bordering the wall.

"Why are you part of the gang?" I asked Federico's good ear after he joined me on the wall.

"I am doing it to become a painter," he said.

"You joined a gang to become a painter?" I asked, puzzled.

"Art pays very little at the beginning."

I still didn't like the idea of being part of a gang, even if the ultimate cause was noble. Do something great and beautiful, the Maestro had said. He didn't say, Go kidnap unhappy dogs. To relax, I pulled out the bottle of Drakkar Noir and pressed it against my lip.

"Do you like being a painter?" I asked.

"Yes, but there's a but," the fourteen-year-old painter said. "I've never painted a girl naked. I'd like to paint a girl naked."

"I would love to buy one of your paintings," I smiled, inebriated. The cologne was already working its magic.

A couple of fireworks lit the sky.

"You have no idea what I'd do to paint Chloé naked. At least her tits. She's cute, right?" said Federico, looking at me.

Now, the sky was dark again. I oddly felt the muscles on my face move.

"And she's pretty smart too. She must have the smartest tits in the world, don't you agree?" he continued excitedly. "Oh, and I think she's into you...didn't you see, she caressed your scar as if it was your penis."

I couldn't help taking another hit of Drakkar Noir. Two fireworks exploded in the sky. A loud sound came from the gate.

"That's the signal!" shouted Federico, adjusting his hearing aid. He jumped down. "You climb over with the dog, I go to the gate."

As I landed on the asphalt with Eugene in my arms, I felt dizzy. The Drakkar Noir—or perhaps it was the conversation with the painter—had left me completely stoned. I felt like I had just smoked ten pounds of marijuana. I was stumbling. The dog was looking at me quizzically.

"No, Eugene," I said, slurring my words. "I don't think she likes me."

As if to contradict me, the Labrador barked and headed across the road. It seemed he wanted to take me somewhere. Well, okay. A stolen family dog leads you on a path, you follow. He sniffed his way, then broke into a run. He dragged me down the hill until we reached an empty spot at the edge of the woods.

The night lit up the tombstones here and there. Some stones were crooked, some straight, and others were yellowish and abandoned. One could make out the etched inscriptions: RUFOLO, 1924–1930; LORD; ORZO, BELOVED FOX TERRIER... It was a little pet cemetery on the edge of the woods that had been there for a hundred years. Back in the early 1900s British aristocracy owned lavish summer homes on the Italian Riviera; they believed that their pets had souls, too, and deserved a quiet place to rest in peace.

Suddenly, the dog stopped in front of a stone. After sniffing some roots he grew calm. The Labrador looked at the stone, as if he were trying to read: LITTLE LIZA PUT TO SLEEP MARCH 6, 2002. Then he howled a long, beautiful serenade.

When I thought of love, I usually thought of Marinella, whom I loved and who was dead; but now I thought of someone else, of someone living.

Don Otto, the Baker

CHLOÉ VERDI

Was Rosso Fiorentino's first idea for the company inspired by market research, his past experience, or his own knowledge of the business?" asked the prosecutor, looking at the magnetic blue flag of the State of New York, which was hanging high above the jury bench. "Or was it inspired by a kiss from you back in Italy, Ms. Verdi?" There was some laughter in the courtroom.

ROSSO FIORENTINO

n ever make a baker angry." This old Italian prov-
erb is engraved on the counter of Don Otto's
bakery. In Italy, bakers are considered more patient
than sages and stronger than boxers; yet last night I
managed to piss off the best one on the Riviera.

When I arrived at the bakery, it was two o'clock
in the morning. In honor of the Madonna of Monte
Allegro, Rapallo's neighborhoods had competed so
doggedly to display the best fireworks that, during
the grand finale, a priest had lost two fingers on a
firecracker that went off early. The air still smelled of
burnt paper. After the harsh sound of the bolt latch,
the bakery's door squeaked open and Don Otto's face
appeared.

"You lost the dog?" he asked.

"He was excited. He managed to rip off the leash,
and ran back to the villa," I said defensively.

"And the police arrived."

I followed Don Otto down to the bakery in the basement. The only light there came from the oven and from the streetlamp spilling through the grating in the ceiling's corner.

"How much do I owe you?" I asked.

"Three hours at the police station," said Don Otto.

"They didn't fine you?"

"Lucky for you, they didn't. Still, we lost good money from an honest ransom. I imagine Chloé is a bit pissed off too."

Without saying anything more, he began to knead. The race against time had started. Don Otto had to bake forty pans of focaccia before the bakery opened at six, and he had lost three hours at the police station. Although he was as large as a piece of baroque furniture, all his energy seemed concentrated in his soft, pink hands. Don Otto was a bit older than us, and he was so strong and fatherly-looking that, had he not been a virgin, you would have liked to be his child.

The twins' arrival interrupted the silence in the bakery.

"Can we have a round of focaccia, please?" said Virginia through the grating with a drunken French r, betraying her Northern Italian royal origin.

I caught a glimpse of panties through the tear of her ripped military trousers. In the baker's trade you see things from the bottom up.

"C'mon, will you please give us a slice?" said Ginevra. "Virginia had too much to drink and she's about to throw up."

A pair of leather driving moccasins of some new arrival came into view. The moccasins had a lift inside them to make the man look taller, his ankles rose visibly out of his shoes.

"Leave it to me, girls!" the new arrival said confidently. "Don Otto, it's me, Renzo Piano. Will you cut us a pound of plain focaccia?"

"We're closed," said Don Otto, unmoved.

"Then what's *he* doing inside?" Ginevra pointed down to me. "Virginia is about to puke."

The sound of thick splatter interrupted the flow of the inquiry.

"Hey, who threw up on my moccasins!" said Renzo Piano.

Like the inner workings of a magic door, the law of the bolt latch was incomprehensible, perhaps even to the baker himself. Sometimes he would let in some random guy like me, and then he would keep out a world-class architect and the twins who belonged to Italy's richest family. People came from all over Italy to try a slice of Don Otto's focaccia.

Suddenly, two kicks shook the grating like a whip on a bare back. This new arrival moved Don Otto to raise his head for the first time.

"Do you want a slice?" he asked, drying his face on his apron with a look of concern.

"No, I want your friend," Chloé said.

I followed her through the narrow streets of Rapallo. The night was cool, almost cold. A strong Ponentino wind was blowing in from the sea. She walked in front of me without saying anything, her swift arms dangling a bit. She was still wearing her orange bikini and her striped T-shirt, which outlined the shape of her breasts.

When we reached the promenade, I noticed there had been a wedding somewhere. Following the Riviera's tradition, two fishermen had entered the sea up to their ankles, and were lighting small red lanterns and placing them in the water, in honor of the bride. The idea was that when the current pulls them out to the Tigulio Sea the water would look like the train of a wedding dress. Funny, every walk with Chloé seemed to lead me to a wedding.

"Here," I said. "To make up for the ransom."

Chloé looked at the piece of paper I'd handed to her. "You're giving me a check?"

"Yes, that is a check," I said. As I pronounced the hard k, I felt a slap across my face. Now my bank account was down again to 600 euros. I had already lost the money I had made by selling the crest.

After slapping me, Chloé slipped the check inside her bikini top, gracefully, as if it were a dandelion. Then she climbed up onto the railing of the promenade and began to walk along it. When she raised her arms for balance, her T-shirt lifted to expose her belly button. It was at my eye level. I walked alongside her, on the ground.

"You know that being a good-for-nothing will lead you to a bad end?" she said.

"You're coming to a bad end, too," I said. "Weren't you an aspiring journalist? Why do you steal?"

"To pay for law school. Franz and I are going to the University of Chicago in the fall. I wonder if you've even heard of it."

It wasn't uncommon. Unemployment was so high in Italy, and schools were so expensive in America, everyone had to steal to pay for tuition in the United States.

"Oh, my mother talks about it all the time," I said. "Finish your degree, get a master's in America, and become president of the United States. Except that if you have to steal to pay for your U.S. tuition, it makes it harder to become president even with a master's." I paused for a moment, reconsidering that. "Or maybe not."

A gust of wind blew out some of the lanterns the fishermen had placed in the sea. Other lanterns were submerged by a wave. It was too windy a night to foster the tradition of the red lanterns.

"If your mother had gone broke paying your medical bills like mine did," Chloé said without looking at me, but I felt the weight of her gaze, "you wouldn't act so spoiled."

The two fishermen, relentlessly, decided to place a second batch of lanterns into the water despite the wind.

"Can you explain to me how you managed to lose the dog?" she asked.

I searched for the words to say something that, in fact, had nothing to do with her question. I was somewhere else. I walked in silence for a bit.

"So?" she asked.

After Marinella and the accident, I had promised myself I would never run after a woman again. And yet I was now standing on the Rapallo promenade with my heart on my sleeves.

"You know that Sachin wrote a book?" I said.

"And what does that have to do with the fact that you lost the dog?" she said impatiently.

"In his book the protagonist searches for his great love, the Venus with the Singing Nipples."

"And what the hell does that have to do with anything?"

I looked to the sea, faltering. "It's you."

"The Venus with the Singing Nipples?" Chloé laughed, lost her balance and landed on the ground. She looked down at her breasts covered by the orange bikini top. "I don't know if they sing...Is this a declaration of love?"

"Yes," I said. "What were you thinking...a tax audit?"

She climbed back onto the railing and continued walking on it. Either the sea breeze or the check had blown away her bad mood. In a mere hour's time, Chloé's eyes had smoldered at me, darkly, then sparkled with a desire so bright it could awaken a white tiger—nothing like the cold, changeless, unreadable eyes of Marinella. Her light tan contrasted with the pale scars along her arms.

At last, it seemed the two fishermen had conquered the wind. They were placing hundreds of red lanterns in the water, which were gently floating out to sea. It was like looking at New York City from an airplane.

"What happened here?" I asked, reaching to touch her arm.

Chloé pulled away and sat down astride the railing in front of me.

"What happened to you?" She said placing her index finger on the scar on my chin and moving it gently. "Is it true that you're a prince?"

"Well, my father sold the title and yesterday I sold a copy of our family crest. We're broke." I couldn't tell if she was more attracted by the fact that I came from a princely family or by the fact that I was broke.

"What happened here on your arms? Are these the medical bills?"

Instead of responding, she kissed me.

She was darting her tongue fast, like a girl kissing for the first time, and I felt as though I was walking into the cold sea up to my navel. She still tasted a bit of focaccia. Then she pulled back and looked at me with her stunning green eyes, now happy.

"He was cool, the Maestro, right?" she said. "You're not so bad yourself. Pity you're a good-for-nothing."

When I returned to the bakery, the sky behind the houses was lit up a faint gray. The crisp scent of dawn was mixed with the warm, oily smell of focaccia permeating the narrow streets.

Don was putting the last pan into the oven. He was working solely with his left hand because his right one was locked in a cramp, his apron drenched with sweat. His face wore the grimace of a she-wolf that has just given birth. The other pans were cooling in front of the grating.

"Don Otto, it must be because you've never fucked anyone that you're such an asshole!" Ginevra shouted, finally grabbing the tray of focaccia Don was handing to her. Then the echo of her boots disappeared at the end of the *caruggio*.

"So what do you think it means?" I asked him.

"Well, if she kissed you it means she's no longer angry," he responded curtly. He didn't like to discuss questions of the heart.

"You've really never fucked, Don?"

"No."

I looked at the pans where the crusts were cooling, the stracchino cheese crackling. I touched my mouth; it still tasted like Chloé.

"Don Otto," I said slowly. "I've got it."

"You've got what?"

"I have a great idea," I said. "We export focaccia to America."

He closed the oven and stood up, without nodding, listening.

"Well?" I said. "Isn't it beautiful?"

"First you call your own idea great, now it's beautiful too?"

"Yes," I said. Though I wasn't sure yet that exporting bread to the United States was along the lines of the Maestro's vision.

"You want to go to America, Primrose?" said Don Otto to the flower he kept over the oven and that he watered lovingly every morning. "No, I don't think that Primrose wants to go to America."

Federico, the Painter

CHLOÉ VERDI

May 4, 2009, New York

What's the first thing Rosso Fiorentino did after he came up with the idea for the company? Did he start diligently working on a business plan, review precedents, run a market analysis... or did he consult a fortune-teller?" There was more laughter in the courtroom.

ROSSO FIORENTINO

July 5, 2006, Rapallo, Italy

After I left the bakery this morning, I walked up to Sant'Ambrogio, where the fourteen-year-old painter lives. It was six-thirty, and I tried not to smile as I walked in the early morning mist. Even so, at times, I nodded at a cypress or did a tip-tap dance between two light-purple bougainvilleas. There was that smell of dry pine needles in the air. I had spent an all-nighter at the bakery but felt like sprinting all the way up the hill.

Federico rented out the second floor of a small orange house that had once belonged to Ezra Pound. Because his parents disapproved of his passion for painting, he had found a way to become financially independent: when he wasn't on ransom-collecting missions with the Octopus Gang, he provided bad-luck removal services in exchange for a generous fee. Besides being a painter, Federico loved the stars. In the third grade, he was already reading books about celestial mechanics and could operate his own telescope. As a result of certain fortunate coincidences, as well as an in-depth knowledge of horoscopes, word eventually spread that in Rapallo there lived a young blond boy who could skillfully remove one's bad luck. Before important exams, especially toward year-end, his fellow fifth graders would stop by to see him. More than once, tennis coach Mario Costa came in from Zoagli to have his tennis balls "greased." People said that in 2003, Genoa, the local soccer team—one of the oldest in Italy—was able to remain in the Second Division thanks to Federico's "oil."

After my car accident, various people suggested that I see a shrink or even an exorcist, to have my alleged bad luck removed—*farmi togliere il malocchio*, as they said. I refused; it seemed cheap to me. But now that I was starting a company, I realized quite reasonably that I needed to have luck on my side.

When I reached the boy painter's house, I saw him through the open windows of his studio. He was already walking in front of his canvas. In just one hand he was holding two thick oxtail brushes, a thin marten one, and a super-thin 0.0 squirrel brush to touch up the details. When I called his name and he didn't answer (as expected; he's deaf), I decided to let myself inside. He was painting a contemporary version of

Saint George and the Dragon. It was impressive to see a fourteen-year-old boy taking so many steps back and forth in front of a canvas. I counted: sixteen steps a minute, a mile per hour.

"I want to be lucky," I said. "But I don't have money to pay you."

"That's okay," Federico said, cleaning his brushes with a cloth soaked in turpentine and then laying them down on the table next to the painting. "If you'll help me take my paintings to the show in Levanto tomorrow, I'll remove your bad luck for free."

He disappeared into and then returned from the kitchen—five square feet in the far corner of his studio—pushing a small tray. I felt as if I were at the dentist when I heard the squeaking of the little wheels on the floor. The tray held a white soup bowl, a bottle of water, pink sea salt, a pair of scissors, a box of matches, and a tiny glass pitcher of his rare and famous oil. Federico had put something on his head—a cross between a doctor's cap and a fedora—so that his curly blond hair wouldn't get in the way. After making some strange movements with his hands and arms, he poured the water into the soup bowl and added two drops of oil. He looked inside.

"Oh yes, you have bad luck," Federico nodded, pointing at the large balls of oil that had congealed at the bottom of the bowl. "Otherwise the oil would be floating up. Let's see what I can do."

He first touched the back of my neck and my forehead. Then he cut off my bad luck with the pair of scissors and lit a match to burn it. Finally, he threw four handfuls of pink sea salt in the water, to prevent the bad luck from growing back.

He peered again into the bowl and shook his head.

"Sorry, man. I wasn't able to take it all out. You've got shitloads of bad luck."

Seeking further remedies, at around seven o'clock in the evening the painter and I went to buy an offering—a bouquet of daisies from the local flower market—and climbed up the hill of Camogli. In severe cases of bad luck, Federico recommended the Christ of the Abyss: a bronze statue built in 1954 that was dropped to the bottom of the sea between Camogli and Portofino, to protect all the shipwrecks around the world. Locals said that if you hoped for something, if you really hoped for something to happen, you should bring an offering to the Christ of the Abyss. Then it usually happens.

When we reached the top of the hill, we quickly undressed and approached the edge of a steep cliff. Federico put on his life jacket. Then he placed two large stones inside my bathing suit, just beside my testicles. The weight of the stones would drag me down to the seabed.

"When you reach the seabed, drop the offering," said Federico.

I looked down below. I felt a knot in my throat. It was a forty-five-foot drop. I adjusted the position of my testicles inside my swimsuit.

"I have to say 'love,' 'fortune,' and all the things I want to be lucky in," I repeated, swallowing each word one by one.

I usually prayed just to relax; I didn't know if this was actually religious or only superstitious. I looked down again. I should actually have been praying to land in one piece. The Mediterranean Sea glittered in the last sun. From where we stood, it looked smaller than a pond.

"And you have to say, 'Find an art dealer,'" said Federico.

"Why? I don't need to find an art dealer."

"I need to find an art dealer."

"Can't you find it with your own magic?" I asked.

The boy shook his head. "He who is his own magician has a fool for a client."

We counted down from ten, then dove into the emptiness side by side. I felt my stomach in my throat, my nose in my toes, and the speed twisted our mouths as if we were cartoons. The sun was big and red and blinded me like a promise of glory.

When we hit the sea, there was an immediate silence. While Federico was pulled up by his life jacket, I kept sinking. The rocks inside my bathing suit dragged me down. The water was lukewarm and bright, and there were all kinds of yellow and red fish around me. Then the current became cooler. The fish were fewer and fewer. I clenched the bouquet of daisies against my chest. Now I was starting to feel dizzy. I felt that pinch inside my lungs.

Finally, from out of the abyss, a beard appeared, then two arms reaching toward the seas and the skies, and then all of the Christ of the Abyss became clear in its infinite whiteness. After dropping the offering at the statue's feet, I swam up.

*A*nd, now you'll find a dealer!" I shouted, coughing up some water. I grabbed on to what I believed were the painter's shoulders to catch my breath.

"Gagosian," nodded Federico, enunciating the name of the biggest New York gallery. I now noticed that he was sitting on a rock.

"Finding a dealer…is that your pickup line?" asked Ginevra, freeing herself from my grasp and splashing me in the face. "Is that how you pick up girls?"

"What are you doing here? I'm sorry, from behind…," I said. From behind I'd thought she was Federico.

"Usually his pickup line is to offer girls a slice of focaccia," Federico said from the rock, laughing.

Another head came up out of the water, next to Ginevra's.

Damn, how long had I been down there? Where did she come from?

"Well, we'd do almost anything for that focaccia," said Virginia, smiling.

A hint of moon suddenly drew a white broken line across the sea. Then the twins went off swimming in a circle like two African dolphins. Again, they failed to recognize me, I thought, relieved. I climbed up the rock Federico was sitting on and sat beside him.

"A portrait of those two would land you a slot at the Venice Biennale," I said. "You may be on to something with your Christ of the Abyss."

Federico was drying his hearing aid, which was full of water. Somehow, even without hearing, he could follow my train of thought.

"That's what I wanted to talk to you about," he said. "You know that I've never painted a girl naked."

"Yes, we need to fix that."

"I would like to paint Virginia naked."

"Okay," I said. I was in the state of mind I had been for the past twenty-four hours where everything seemed easy. Export foccacia to the United States? Have your bad luck removed by a fourteen-year-old boy? Dive into an abyss to meet the Christ? Anything was possible.

The two girls had changed behind a rock and were now jumping from boulder to boulder, holding their wet bathing suits in one hand.

"Come on, guys, let's go have focaccia!" shouted Ginevra. Focaccia! A convincing display of the beauty of my great idea.

When we arrived on the promenade, it was deserted except for a single pair of forgotten sandals. The night was blue and inspiring. In the twilight, the twins dried their hair, bending their necks to one side, squeezing the tips of their curls. The dirty sweet smell of focaccia was already emanating from Don Otto's bakery.

I knocked at the door a few times and eventually Don let us in. I ordered for everybody.

Virginia took two slices, one for herself and one for her sister, then quickly and expertly closed the wrapper to keep the bread warm, while Federico passed around flyers for his upcoming show.

"See, that sexually retarded baker does sell focaccia to you!" said Ginevra

"How can we thank you?" said Virginia, looking at me, smiling, her mouth full, her fingers greasy.

"Federico would like to paint you naked," I said.

"My friend is joking," said Federico blushing.

Virginia laughed, coughed, almost choked, revealing two small slightly crooked canines. In addition to being the richest in Italy, her family had one of the largest art collections in the world.

"Totally naked?" she asked taking a deep breath. "Damn. I didn't think a slice of Don Otto's focaccia could be so expensive!"

I stayed at Federico's that night; the next morning we had to leave early for the art show. I lay down on a blue chaise longue, which occupied most of Federico's studio, and started writing. The windows were open, and in came the inebriating smell of garlic fields from the hills. The words were lining up on the page as if of their own accord.

Federico was painting on the terrace, next to his telescope. Now and then he drank a shot of yellow grappa. Although he had started painting at seven that morning and the grappa was 140 proof and he was only fourteen, his stroke was clean, without interruptions, like the trail of an airplane that's only just passed by.

As he moved back and forth in the dark in front of his canvas, however, the painting itself began to take a different shape than he'd intended. Maybe because he was upset about something I had said. He wanted his Saint George to be strong and athletic, and to prevail over the dragon according to tradition. Yet at each brushstroke the dragon grew stronger, the scales on the neck looked sharper, its claws thicker and invincible, while the more he dotted the saint's armor, the sloppier and more listless his Saint George became, until he was all bunched up over himself.

"I asked you to help me get a dealer, not make me look like an idiot!" shouted Federico at me from the terrace.

"If you want, I can put in a good word with Chloé as well," I said.

"Oh, don't brag. Besides, she'll end up with Franz."

I suddenly felt as if the dragon's tail had whacked me in the face. All the euphoria of the day vanished.

"It's not going to fly with her," said the painter. "She's way out of your league."

"Because she graduated at twenty-two and I'm one exam short?"

"Come on, Rosso. It's a long time you're one exam short."

When we arrived in Levanto the next morning, the sky was dark gray and the sea was as rough as in November. We had to rent a Ducato minivan because Federico liked to paint immense surfaces and his canvases did not fit inside a regular car. If he could have, he would have painted the entire Torino-Savona Expressway (320 miles). Federico was so nervous during the ride to Levanto, he kept adjusting his hearing aid, which wouldn't stop whistling.

As I scrambled to arrange Federico's paintings, imagining how a bona fide art mover would do this, the painter's words from the night before continued to echo in my ears. *She's out of your league.* Once upon a time, to make an impression on girls, you had to be invited to parties. Now it is all much less dignified, it's all about salaries. If Franz is a better match, it's because he's on his way to being paid telephone numbers. How can you reduce a person to a bunch of numbers? As a response, a large explosion came from the van's engine. The trunk's door landed a few feet away, together with one of Federico's paintings.

"Shit! Did you fuel it with gasoline instead of diesel?" Federico said, turning to me. "Either you're an idiot or you still have bad luck."

I said nothing to that.

While I was unloading what remained of the van, Mr. Carlito Fragola, the curator of the show, measured the paintings. He was Federico's art school teacher and, on the side, organized shows to turn a small profit. He was a man in his early fifties, and wore a cotton jacket and had a ruddy face with frail brown eyes. I'm not sure I liked him. You could have put him in front of a canvas or a corpse and his facial expression would have been exactly the same. He didn't seem to like art—maybe because it paid him little money—and he particularly disliked the grand figurative canvases like Federico's because they were impossible to sell. What paid some bucks was conceptual art, which was now fashionable. He still had to allow Federico's paintings to join the group show, as it was open to all of the school's students.

"Where's the gallery?" I asked.

"Via Magenta is the gallery," Federico said, pointing to the sidewalk and the concrete. "Better to start on the street and end up at the Louvre than vice versa."

I browsed the other artwork on display, none of which seemed in tune with Federico's large oil canvases: a Marlboro cigarette attached to a string; a T-shirt with a Lacoste crocodile crying; a perfectly white surface with a stain of Marmite on it.

"No figurative representation. We only show conceptual work here," said the curator, grimacing at Federico's Saint George and the Dragon. "You have nothing smaller?"

"The smallest is 460 by 240," said Federico.

"Then you may only show one painting."

Around five in the afternoon the first visitors began to arrive: the old men on their way to their first Negroni; kids, returning from the seaside, pretending as a joke to step on the artwork with their wet feet encrusted with sand; some fortune-tellers, friends of Federico's. They all seemed absolutely uninterested, like the curator.

At times, a visitor would ask for the sake of asking something, "Which artists are promising? Anyone in particular?"

"Well, everyone...," repeated the curator while idly rotating his raised hand. Then suddenly his hand splayed open.

At the end of Via Magenta there was a small traffic jam as the dark midnight-blue Maserati drove in. A bus had slammed on the brakes. The riders on mopeds, which could pass on the right, slowed down in an attempt to peer inside the dark-tinted windows. The old men stopped to watch too.

"Did *Flash Art* run a piece on the show?" asked a surprised visitor.

"Fuck, it looks more like *Vanity Fair*!" the curator said flabbergasted.

After an imperceptible bow, the twins stepped out of the Maserati. Their appearance at a show, in Italy as elsewhere, meant the attention of journalists, who constantly followed them. And from out of nowhere, two reporters from *La Stampa* were already taking snapshots with their iPhones.

The teenaged girls began walking slowly in front of the artwork, their hands behind their backs. They were standing right there, yet at the same time seemed totally out of reach; they were glancing at everything, yet without stopping in front of any piece. The curator excitedly followed them, asking questions nonstop,

"Would your father like this one? Wouldn't that make sense in his Damien Hirst collection?" He seemed to have rediscovered a love for the arts. "But why are you going so fast?" Walking straight past cigarettes on a string, the crying Lacoste, and the rest of that bizarre assembly of pieces, the twins were taking a second tour. "If I may…," the curator went on, "It's all about conceptual art nowadays." To his surprise, Virginia slowed down in front of the only painting in the show.

She moved her glance from the pale, defeated face of the saint to the green eyes of the triumphant dragon. Suddenly she froze. Her cheeks betrayed a blush of color. She wiped her chin with her hand. Did the dragon just kiss her? The curator nodded. "Of course, figurative—it's the new conceptual."

Virginia, or Saving Dad

CHLOÉ VERDI

May 4, 2009, New York City

In modern capitalism, beneath any great fortune lies a crime. In fact, here we have a plethora. But do tell us, Miss Verdi," the prosecutor said, his eyes shining, "what are the skeletons in Rosso Fiorentino's closet?"

ROSSO FIORENTINO

July 5, 2006, Portofino, Italy

When Virginia bought Federico's painting at the art show, she slipped a note inside his hand. "Do you still want to paint me?" Although the note didn't specify when or where, or even if it was a joke, the fourteen-year-old unilaterally decided that he would go see Virginia that same night.

At around nine o'clock, we approached the villa by sea in a green rowboat we had rented at the harbor. It was a windless evening. The only lights to guide us came from the dim lamps on the Piazzetta of Portofino; the villa's park was already dark, but I knew it by heart. It was here where I had spent many summers with Marinella's family, including the twins, when they were little. The park occupied the entire hill. It started up there, at the top of the hill, by an anonymous rusty gate, passing through the cypresses' garden labyrinth—at the center of which (according to the evil tongues) was the statue of one of the patriarch's mistresses; it then passed a hidden swimming pool, which had been built for some grandmother (as per the etiquette, at the seaside there should be no pool, and if there is one it should be invisible), and it bordered the tennis court (the park's belly button) before winding all the way down for another two hundred feet to the *spiaggetta*, the private beach.

"I don't want to break inside that villa," I said. "It brings back bad memories."

I told him about Marinella.

"If you really want to get rid of your bad spell, if you want to move forward, you have to look backward," Federico said. "You have to deal with your past."

I tied the boat to a large rock covered in yellow seaweed. The fourteen-year-old painter stretched out his hand so that I could help him jump off, but he dragged me straight into the sea with him.

"Fuck, Rosso! I told you that deaf people have no balance..."

Completely soaked, we began walking up the large imperial staircase. There were 999 steps to reach the top of the hill. I started to count them, and at each step, a different memory came flying back.

Steps 1–15: Grandmother Margherita sitting down on the terrace for lunch at two o'clock sharp on a bright July day. She had a glass of Pimm's to her right, with a thick slice of peach. On the white linen tablecloth, the forks' glittering tines were facedown, since the family insignia was engraved on the back. The fork teeth were curved and smooth, just like the bay of Portofino.

Steps 27–35: Grandmother Margherita looking around, a transparent smile for everyone and everything her gaze landed on, but only for a second: the young waiter who was dressing the salad; Cherry, her fox terrier, barking at something; and the twins, Virginia and Ginevra, in their white summer sailor suits with blue stripes, *vestite alla marinara*, joining the children's table at the far corner of the terrace.

Steps 47–59: The nannies would arrive and sit at the children's table too, trying to be as invisible as possible. Then Giovanni's children would arrive, then Clemente's, Edoardo's, Clara's, and Laura's. It was easier to find your way in Henry VIII's garden labyrinth than into this family tree, which included more than sixty-four first cousins.

Steps 66–69: Finally Grandmother Margherita's two sons would arrive, Clemente and Giovanni, the patriarch. Yes, thirteen months' age difference would make one the patriarch—the head of a business empire and to some extent of a country—and the other one just "the brother." Clemente would often initiate the bickering by inquiring after each family company's performance. "How's cement doing, Giovanni?" "Only 99 percent pure," the patriarch, known for his dark humor, would answer—an allusion to the custom of burying enemies in cement, where their body parts made up the remaining 1 percent. "Cement is doing better than our banks, and the banks are doing better than our newspapers, but not too many checks are coming this way these days," Clemente summarized.

Steps 69–70: "And where's Marinella?" Giovanni would ask, demanding his favorite daughter.

Steps 70–97: Of course Marinella was late.

Steps 102–108: As usual, Giovanni, the patriarch, was wearing a red Battistoni tie with his light linen suit, and his white hair framed his boyish, regal face. Its stillness expressed, at the same time, an extraordinary selfishness and that slight melancholy of those who aren't allowed to have feelings. He had collected as many successes in business as losses in his private life. He did not know how to hug a child, and he had never done it, yet a joke of his would make the Stock Exchange roar or tumble. When he squinted, his wrinkles gathered around his tanned cheeks, like a group of teenagers in front of an ice cream parlor.

Steps 113–234: "Come in...," Marinella had said. This was the first time I'd met her. I pushed open the half-shut door to the room from which her voice came. A cigarette lay burning in an ashtray. Once in a while she put it to her mouth and squeezed it between her lips, and two white dense columns of smoke issued from her nostrils, as if from those of a dragon. But she was the most beautiful dragon.

Steps 247–316: Our first dance. "And what about Franz?" I asked. "That again! Are you in love with him?" Marinella said laughing. "I like someone else." "Whom?" I dared to ask. "You really are a bit thick!" she said, and kissed me. "Whom do you think?" she asked embarrassed. I was staring at her unreadable eyes, her chapped lips, and the tiara shining on her white forehead. And I couldn't believe it.

Steps 397–435: The only time we ever made love. "You've changed," Marinella said, looking at me. "I did it for you. You for the better and I for the worse," I said, smiling. And we made love. I could hear her heart beat, the beautiful, steady rhythm of her heart. I held her big toes as if they were the buttons that piloted the world.

Step 666: Franz's warning. "You shall not desire your neighbor's wife. You took her from me, someone will take her from you."

Steps 667–690: Our last party. On the top floor, two blue spotlights from the Orient Express illuminated a gold bathtub. We began to spin around the dining room table hand in hand. We spun around for hours and my temperature was rising. "You're sick, let's go home!" Marinella said, taking my hand. "Come on, let's go home and make love again!" The guests were singing.

Steps 690–998: Marinella was sitting by my side in the car. My vision was blurred. Badly lit curves disappearing into the dining room tablecloth. A dark street unrolling in front of me and, at the same time, the bubbly amber of the champagne. The waiters under the hot chandelier uncorked new bottles. It seemed like the corks were rolling around the asphalt. Then the punch spilled and the wheels skidded. The pitcher began to roll and the brakes locked. The steering wheel, like a chicken thigh, flew out of my hand. In half a second, the car slammed against the guardrail, reared up, and flew into the air. When it landed everything was quiet.

Step 999: There was a pound of brain matter on the asphalt.

Without realizing it, I had reached the top of the hill. I was standing in front of the statue in the garden labyrinth in honor of the patriarch's mistress. He had built a business empire and a country, while I had taken Marinella from him, and then from the world, with a wrong turn. Can I do worse?

W hat are you doing here?" Virginia asked the fourteen-year-old painter, opening wide her bedroom windows.

Federico was standing on the balcony of her room, still dripping, holding his satchel. We had managed to avoid the Dobermans that were barking excitedly at the moon and climbed up the kitchen's gutters. I knew the route. While Federico presented himself, I hid inside a secret closet that connected the bathroom to two other chambers: Virginia's bedroom and the room that once had been Marinella's. I had hidden so many times inside that closet playing hide-and-seek, or spying on girls getting changed, that I knew the cracks in the wood by heart. The smell of mothballs and vinegar was ever the same.

"You'd rather we do it another time?" Federico asked.

"Now that you're here, you may as well dry yourself," Virginia replied, throwing a towel in his face.

Then she walked back inside her bedroom, leaving the window open.

"Thanks for coming today," Federico said, following her inside, and somehow managing to slip out of his wet pants even as he walked. Near his navel, his tanned stomach still seemed to give off the heat from the sun. "You should have seen the curator's face when you both arrived."

"Shouldn't I be the one stripping down to my underwear?" Virginia laughed. She was now sitting at the head of the long table that occupied her room. She wore a white linen shirt, on which her father's initials were embroidered in dark blue thread, and a pair of white pants with tortoise-shell buttons. Her room had almost no decorations or clutter of any kind, except for a backgammon table whose pieces suggested an interrupted game.

She stretched her fingers and crumpled the table-cloth slightly. "I want you to paint my hands."

After searching in his folder for a sheet that wasn't wet, Federico began drawing. Although his stroke was typically clean and smooth, even when he drank an entire bottle of 140-proof grappa, that night his pencil seemed alive, bouncing in his hands like a techno dancer.

"What do you want to be when you grow up?" Virginia asked, snatching the unfinished drawing out of Federico's hands. She looked at it attentively without saying anything. She had moved the chair so that he could sit next to her.

"I want to be a painter," said the painter. "And you?"

"Promise not to laugh," said the sixteen-year-old girl, weighing a backgammon piece in her hand. She looked Federico in the eye. "You see, there are many fathers who want to save their children. I want to do the opposite. I want to save my father."

"Why, what's wrong with him?"

"He's unhappy."

"I'd save my sister, if I wasn't an only child," said Federico. "My father's a ball buster."

Virginia turned the backgammon piece over in her hand. Suddenly her eyes were a darker blue, almost violet, and seemed to be looking at a distant object. Then she put down the backgammon piece and distractedly pulled out two bills from a desk and handed them to Federico as payment for the drawing.

"My older sister, Marinella," said Virginia. "She died in a car accident."

Through the closet door's crack, I felt my own breath. I thought she was looking right at me.

Federico restored one of the bills to the table. "I only charge one hundred per drawing. I'm sorry, I didn't mean to upset you."

How could he forget, how could he fuck up so badly? I had told him about Marinella. Or maybe it wasn't a fuckup at all?

"What do you want to do when you grow up?" Virginia asked herself. "I want to be a lawyer, a journalist, an acrobat... And you, what about you? I want to save Dad..."

As if she were trying to chase away unpleasant thoughts, Virginia performed a few ballet steps in the room, just as Marinella had done the first time I met her. Virginia stretched her arms and kicked her legs haphazardly, in her white pants with the tortoise-shell buttons. Then she took the painter by the hand.

"As requested... Here, to thank you for the focaccia...," Virginia said leaning against the wall. She closed her eyes as if she were standing before an imaginary firing squad. Then she loosened her shirt, exposing two ivory breasts. "Are we even now?"

Federico looked for another pencil because this one continued to dance in his hand like a techno dancer gone crazy.

"Didn't we say naked?" he found the courage to say.

Virginia undid the first tortoise-shell button of her pants. On her stomach there was a buttery, golden glow of after-sun lotion. The swimsuit tan lines appeared, then the panties' elastic. With a single gesture, she took off the rest. Federico's hand was now trembling so much that you had no idea what the hell he was drawing.

As she walked naked across the room, her image became larger and larger within the crack in the wood until she came to where I was. I could now hear her breathing behind the wood. Or was the breath mine? Then the closet's copper handle turned, and the door opened wide.

"Why are you hiding?" she asked me.

Chicago Boys

CHLOÉ VERDI

May 4, 2009, New York City

F inally in America! Where you came to cause so much trouble," said the prosecutor, twirling his pen and looking at me. "So how does one get to be hired by the best Wall Street firm, Ms. Verdi? How did you become a Chicago boy?"

CHLOÉ VERDI

September 2006–May 2007, Chicago

Yes, I, Chloé Verdi from Genoa, Italy, I made it all the way to the world's number one university for Nobel prizes... and for suicides per semester.

We shuffled awkwardly past some severe portraits of the Seventh Circuit judges and walked into our classroom at Chicago Law on our first day. The other students were all dressed casually in shorts and sneakers, and yet something about each of them—a grimace, a trait, a tic—suggested that they had passed many selection processes to get here: the small whip in Ferdinand Calice's smile, Mauricio's fingers that jotted down notes faster than a Dictaphone. Only Shimoto's face seemed too nice to be that of a future lawyer.

"One day you'll be partners in a law firm, Nobel prize winners, prime ministers," said Professor Leifsteen walking into our classroom. "But you'll always be Chicago boys. Now let's get straight to work. Let's see..."

As the professor moved his finger around, we all held our breath.

"Mr. Celestri," he said, pointing to the last row. "Mr. Franz Celestri."

We breathed out, relieved, and some students turned to examine the unfortunate one who had been called on...yes, Franz, once known as the master of parties, had made it to the University of Chicago too. Can you imagine we ended up in the same class? He was waiting for the professor to phrase his question but didn't seem too concerned. The master of parties sat as comfortably as if he were sipping a sherry at a black-tie ball.

"What's corporate governance law all about, Mr. Celestri?" Professor Leifsteen asked. The question would have been even more intimidating had I known he had invented this area of law, back in the seventies. "Tell me in your own words."

"It was meant to prevent big, bad companies from doing big, bad stuff," said Franz.

"Correct. So, what's its purpose in more legal terms?"

"It's useless."

There was a moment of complete silence in the classroom. The professor seemed taken aback. Nobody had ever dared to say such a thing to him in thirty years. Not even Congress. Of course, he didn't really mind when smart students challenged his theories.

"Interesting point of view, Mr. Celestri...," he resumed. "Let's see..., Ms. Chloé Verdi?"

I jumped in my seat. Now the class turned to look at me, the girl in the third row, feeling a bit too young and too tanned compared with the rest of the classroom. I lowered my eyes to my pen.

"What recent act introduced corporate governance into law, Ms. Verdi?" the professor asked.

Forty seconds went by. In Italy I had never heard anything about corporate governance.

"I wouldn't know," I said.

"Anybody?" The professor turned to two law students seated in the front but nobody volunteered. He looked again to the last row. "Let's see if Mr. Celestri can answer this one. What act introduced corporate governance into law?"

"The Sarbanes Oxley Act of 2002," answered Franz, "a federal law passed to fight back against major corporate and accounting scandals, such as Enron and WorldCom."

"That is correct. Would you say that the Sarbanes Oxley Act is useless too?" asked the professor provocatively.

Franz took a moment before responding.

"The Securities and Exchange Commission was meant to add teeth to the act."

"But?" asked the professor, sensing an objection in Franz's voice.

"But it's just mouthwash. It might happen all over again, and worse this time."

"Let's hope you don't get an A in corporate governance, Mr. Celestri... for the sake of the U.S. economy."

After class I headed toward the cafeteria. With books under my arm and my hair bouncing on the backpack, I felt that pleasant sense of protection one feels as a student. It was almost noon. I turned around one more time to take it all in. I still couldn't believe I was there. The tinted windows surrounding the fountains shone in the already mild sun. From the outside, the University of Chicago was a black crystal cube that, like the finest minds, was dark by day and lit by night.

I walked by the Rockefeller-endowed buildings. The lawns were damp and the squirrels' voluminous tails curled and stretched in the late September air. Then I exhaled—or was it a sigh? I'd come all the way there to be one-upped by Franz, the master of parties. I don't know why I smiled. Even though I hadn't managed to answer in class, I was in a good mood.

No, I didn't know whether I wanted to be a lawyer or some kind of CEO when I grew up. But I'd always wanted this: to get into a U.S. grad school. Here lay the promise of the tallest skyscrapers, stolen kisses at dawn, salaries as long as telephone numbers. And especially, the possibility of doing something worthwhile.

When I reached the cafeteria, my roommate, Juncal, was outside waiting for me. She was a fun party girl from Madrid—just who I needed as a friend to loosen up a bit. She had ginger-red hair and murdered the English *r*. Unlike the other students, she was studying law not to get to Wall Street but to join a volunteer organization in Tajikistan.

"Are you coming tonight?" she asked me.

"I have to finish reading corporate governance."

"Chloé, remember, pleasure before duty!" She raised her index finger. "With only one exception: always wear your panties."

I laughed. "And why is that necessary?"

"So you don't miss the pleasure of someone taking them off."

I laughed again. Then I shrugged my shoulders. "I hope I can make it. I read English even more slowly than Shimoto."

"You can't read more slowly than Shimoto," said Juncal. "He reads like a turtle races."

After a quick lunch, I went right back to the library. I had to study hard if I wanted to find a job; there was no way around it. We had been assigned a hundred pages of reading on corporate governance, and I decided to study with Shimoto. I felt I had something in common with him, beyond the fact that we both read English slowly.

Shimoto was from Seoul and, like me, had undergone great trials to get into the University of Chicago. His mother had sold the family's land to pay for his tuition. Beneath Shimoto's woolen cap, one could see he had a gentle smile. He wore that cap all the time, as if he wanted to shield his thoughts from the rest of the world.

"Let's grab some A's," I said as I entered the library, handing Shimoto a cup of coffee from the cafeteria. Then I dropped my backpack on an empty table by the window and pulled out some plastic bags. Due to my various allergies, I always carried a pharmacopeia with me. "Chloé's Turkish coffee." I smiled as I melted small pieces of dark Colombian chocolate into his cup, two spoons of sugar, and one of cayenne pepper. "Trust me, it's like gasoline."

"Will that make me a Mazda?" the Korean student smiled back, bringing the drink to his lips.

I looked around with pleasure at the noon sun beating down on the stacks. Studying in the D'Angelo Library, with its broad tables and the windows facing the fountains—it made you feel extraordinarily smart.

Little by little the white sunlight turned to gold and chased down the stacks farther away. For an hour or so it lingered on the Wisconsin Penal Code. Soon enough the fluorescent lamps switched on and drew dark circles beneath the round tables. We had been sitting and reading for close to twelve hours.

Around midnight Harold, the guard, anxious to close the library, shouted, "It's time to go find your parties! Don't you guys have a life?"

His key ring banged against his big belly as he walked away.

I snapped my book shut and called it a day. I pinched my friend on the back of his neck. "Are you coming?"

Shimoto was still leaning on his book. He didn't even get up to pee. He pressed his fingers against his cheeks, so firmly his phalanxes trembled. Damn, what had I given him? Weird sounds came out of his mouth.

W hen I headed back to the International House, my dorm, it was late. There were parties going on all around me. Pity I wasn't invited to any. I could feel the resounding beat of the music even on the sidewalk outside. What a drag I was. And now I had also lost my way.

A silhouette on the other side of the road caught my eye. "Excuse me, do you know which way I-House is?" I asked.

The silhouette looked like a man's, and it was pushing a bicycle toward the crosswalk. He must have been at one of the parties because he was wearing a mask. The temperature had dropped. I felt the cold air suddenly increase; rolling fog banks were enveloping the gutters.

"You don't remember where you live?" The cyclist lifted his mask.

I winced. "If I don't know what corporate governance is, do you expect me to know where I live?" I asked.

"Yes, the two things do usually go together," said Franz, laughing while pushing his bicycle. "Come on, I'll take you to I-House."

We walked past Victor's Pub and the cloying smell of microwave pizza that came from the back door; we passed the damp lawns and the university's black crystal cube, lit now from inside, where, if one listened closely, you could hear the quiet singing of a solitary Korean student. We walked in silence in the cold, our breath preceding us. Franz's breath was calm and steady; mine was short and irregular and embarrassed. He'd outwitted me on our first day of class, and now he was even showing me the way back to my own dorm. I would have liked to kick him right back to Rapallo.

A little flame of pride flared up in me just as we were passing by the medical school. Two figures were turned toward the ferns beside the brick building.

"Hey guys," I called, trying to catch their attention. "Is either of you headed toward I-House?"

"But I'm taking you," said Franz.

"No, you're not," one of the two figures said.

Just then the other one suddenly spun around, displaying a six-inch blade. "Cough up your watch and wallet, man," he said. "And you, sweetheart, what have you got for us?"

Franz made a move to reach for his wallet when all at once, for no reason, the blade went in and out of him, long, cold, and fast.

One evening near the end of January, a group of handpicked students flew out of Chicago and landed at New York's La Guardia Airport. A light rain slicked the pavement as we boarded the bus and gazed out at the approaching city. If for some, like me, getting into Chicago was a lifetime goal, the purpose for attending was right there, beyond the bus windows: the New York Job Fair. I had no idea why I was invited to participate. I had studied hard, but my grades were barely average. Was it because I was female? We stared at the dark and silent East River, at the columns of smoke rising from the Triborough Bridge, and suddenly the patchwork of lights of the Manhattan skyscrapers, inaccessible, splendid, but with a hole in the middle, like a smile without front teeth, and we all were asking ourselves the same thing: will I find a job or will I go home up to my ears in debt?

Some students, like Shimoto, hadn't even gotten an interview, hadn't even gotten this far. I had helped him draft application letters to six potential law firms, but his first-quarter grades were too low. The day when we went together to mail the letters, he knelt in front of the post office sign. "Are you praying to the god of jobs?" I asked smiling. I remember that in response he looked at me and pressed his fingers against his face so hard that a trickle of blood dripped down his cheeks.

That evening in New York, Juncal and I checked in at the Edison, a cheap Broadway hotel between the two last surviving peep shows in all of Manhattan, and went out to look for a restaurant. The rain magnified the lights on Sixth Avenue. It was nice to cross Broadway on the way to the East Side, and smell kebabs, grilled peppers, and caramel almonds, and to brush against businessmen getting out of work, super fat women with pink bags of see-through lingerie, and to feel the whir of the cabs, of the rickshaws, of the bicycles driving on the wrong side of the road. I already felt a part of all of it.

After a forty-five-minute wait, we were seated in the back room at JG Melon's, a burger joint on Seventy-fourth and Third where the customer is always wrong. Since Juncal was leaving in June for Tajikistan, she had come to New York just to eat Melon's mozzarella in carrozza—i.e., grilled cheese sandwiches.

"Let's see ...," I said, looking at the menu intensely, as if it were a curriculum vitae. We had been advised to practice for our interviews, asking one another the standard questions that might come up the day after. "Ms. Juncal, where do you see yourself in five years' time?"

Juncal stretched her arms, smiling. "In the Bahamas." She wasn't participating in the job fair and was not taking the exercise seriously.

"You're not helpful," I said.

"I know. How many interviews do you have?" asked Juncal, laughing, although she knew the answer.

"Two."

"Well, the second one is with SL&B. Why don't you let Franz help you? Don't you know him from back in Italy?"

I lowered my eyes. Slowly, I split the mozzarella sandwich in two. The curtain of warm cheese parted. "This joke is even less funny than the one about the Bahamas."

I remembered that night in late September. Why was I such a poor loser, so petty only because he outsmarted me in class? Had I not spoken to those guys...

"Right," said Juncal, reading my mind. "If it had been me, instead of sending Franz to the hospital I would have shagged him."

The following morning I spent at least an hour staring at the blueberry muffins on the elegant buffet of the Palm Tree Hotel's reception room, where the job fair was taking place.

Oddly, my two interviews were with firms that were ranked on opposite ends of the Lawyer 500 ranking. The first was a small, unknown Wisconsin practice and the second was the Wall Street giant Sinclair, La Touche & Buvlovski.

I had chosen my attire carefully: a knee-length skirt and a green blouse that matched my eyes.

When I proceeded to the twenty-third floor of the Palm Tree Hotel, the candidate interviewed before me was still inside. The rain had stopped and out the window the Morgan Stanley building was clothed in mist. Unlike the other firms' suites, SL&B's reception room boasted no flowers or promotional videos. There was only a somber Copperplate Gothic sign that read Sinclair, La Touche & Buvlovski.

As I waited for my turn, I looked out at that ghost-like edifice.

"Break a leg . . . ," said a voice behind me.

"I think I've done enough damage already!" I laughed, surprised, recognizing a familiar voice. "How did your interview go?"

Franz smiled. "I don't know. Buvlovski isn't easy."

If Franz said the lawyer wasn't easy, it meant he was a bulldog.

"How are you doing?" I asked.

I hadn't spoken to him since the night I'd accompanied him, bloodied, to the emergency room. I had my friends check up on him a couple of times and bring him food and books and even a feel-better sunflower, but I never mustered the courage to visit him myself. When he returned to class, I tried to be invisible.

"Does it still hurt?" I asked.

"No, it's healed." Cavalierly, Franz pushed his jacket flaps aside and lifted his shirt to show me the stitches on his hip. He looked thinner and a bit pale but otherwise unscathed. As ever, he wore the knot in his tie disrespectfully loose.

The suite was large and almost empty. There were only two chairs in the room, placed side by side before a window that looked out on Sixth Avenue. I was not invited to sit, but decided to anyway, and was soon joined by my interviewer. Bumping into Franz had completely broken my concentration.

"Interesting attire, Ms. Chloé Ombra Allegra Verdi...," said Dimitri Buvlovski, looking down from my bright-green blouse to my résumé. "You completed high school in one year and university in thirty-six months, and you graduated cum laude. Surprising, Ms. Verdi. Was it dedication or impatience?"

The lawyer raised his round, bulging eyes from the résumé, waiting for an answer.

"There's nothing wrong with impatience if the grades are cum laude, Ms. Verdi. Unfortunately..." Dimitri Buvlovski got up from his chair and walked across the room. SL&B was the only firm on Wall Street whose managing partner had attended the job fair. Between his raw wool suit, his black sneakers, and the way he dragged his left leg—it was five inches longer than his right one—you wouldn't have guessed he was the highest-paid lawyer on Wall Street. He pulled out a contract from his briefcase and handed it to me.

"Unfortunately?" I asked.

"Unfortunately, in Chicago your grades have not been cum laude," said Buvlovski. "Actually, they are below average. Any comments?"

"Well, usually, the first quarter is the most difficult one," I said. "And Chicago's grade average is B minus."

"No. I meant any comments regarding the contract I just handed you, Ms. Verdi."

After opening the document, which was as thick as an Argentine steak, I began to read it without knowing where to start. SL&B was the only firm on Wall Street that would put applicants through a strenuous test during an interview. Several minutes passed.

"Any comments on the purchase price adjustment clause, Ms. Verdi?" Buvlovski asked.

I bent over the reps and warranties, the covenants, and then the purchase price adjustment formula. The provisions seemed to spin in a circle that I couldn't stop. Instead my head was elsewhere, far away, at the sea of Rapallo, and the day the response from Chicago arrived, and my mother's cry of joy, "You made it!" And now all was at stake. Why couldn't I say anything?

"Thanks, Ms. Verdi," Buvlovski said, retrieving the contract. "Our interview is over."

At the beginning of April, forecasts still predicted that a cold spell was about to arrive and that the wind off Lake Michigan would bend the skyscrapers. Spring came instead. In front of I-House the geraniums bloomed and some students were training outdoors for the university's soccer tournament. The graduating students who had found jobs on Wall Street could relax, enjoy jazz music in the bars, and see the Renoirs at the Art Institute or plan a weekend away in New York to look for an apartment. The others, like me, who hadn't received an offer, sat hungrily and slightly panicked at the library's tables consuming civil procedure manuals, Red Bulls, and my Turkish coffee.

When final grades came out, it was an evening in early May. The lawns were being watered by the sprinklers and smelled of wet grass. I walked back to the library where, in the heat of my finals, I had left my backpack. Since I hadn't received a job offer, I felt the aimlessness of someone who didn't know what she'd do tomorrow. K&J sent me a rejection letter and Sinclair, La Touche & Buvloski did not even bother to answer, though my final grades were above average, between B plus and A minus.

Since there was nothing more I could do, I was going to take a holiday for the night. In fact, I was going out with Franz for the first time. I wondered if he'd make a move and thought, climbing the library's steps, well, if he doesn't, I will.

Harold, the guard, was standing inside the library, right behind the door. He opened the door a crack.

"I left my mascara upstairs," I said, smiling at him proudly. "Harold, I have a date tonight."

But something in the guard's somber eyes told me that this time my smile wasn't going to work. Harold was holding the key ring tight against his large belly without smiling. On the street, the wail of a siren interrupted the hum of the library's air conditioner.

"You don't need mascara, Chloé," said Harold kindly.

The siren stopped. Two paramedics jumped out of the ambulance and ran through the door, which

Harold held open for them. The ambulance's lights were making silent yellow circles in the night.

"What happened?" I asked.

In clockwork intervals the flashing lights lit shards of broken glass on the sidewalk.

"He threw his laptop from the fourth floor," Harold said. "It took three of us to prevent him from jumping."

I felt something lodge inside my throat.

The library door opened once more. On a wheeled stretcher lay a small body. When the stretcher passed in front of me, I noticed that the cuts on his face were deep and his cheeks were all bloodied. He was strapped down to the gurney in full restraints. His brown eyes were staring at me, as if he wanted to tell me something. I came closer.

"Failed!" Shimoto said, smiling.

· JOB 8 ·

The Venus with the

Singing Nipples

CHLOÉ VERDI

May 4, 2009, New York City

W ho was actually in charge of the finances at the company?" asked the prosecutor. "Yes, Ms. Verdi, let's take a step back. Can we hear more about Sachin, the future accountant of the company, and his 'creative' past?"

ROSSO FIORENTINO

September 5–6, 2007, Portofino, Italy

While I continued struggling with a hundred pages of an incomplete novel, a small publishing house from Genoa, Cesar Publishing, had decided to publish the book Sachin had written in one month.

The launch of *The Venus with the Singing Nipples* took place on July 17 at Canepa, a pastry shop in Rapallo, and gained a number of local reviews (on the Web sites Seagullnews.com and NotOnlyTigulio.com, and in the magazine the *Maritime Voice*). Every time an article on his book came out, Sachin would climb up the hills to a hidden restaurant called Ca' Del Frate and order the best Fiorentina steak and a bottle of Vermentino. As he felt the night breeze on his cheeks, warmed by the wine, he would read the review again and again. He couldn't believe that he had written a book, and that the critics said that it was crisp and beautiful (and a bit deranged), and he was beginning to discover his own vanity. Not even in his wildest dreams, however, much less my own, would Sachin have imagined himself at the Italian Book Awards a few months later.

When Federico and I arrived at the Benedictine Abbey of the Cervara for the event, it was the end of a summer evening. The clouds formed a nice row of signs in the sky, like the instructions for a wire transfer. As always, the Book Awards ceremony was held at this famous abbey, trodden upon for thousands of years by monks and now by writers. Sachin was already sitting right on the stage between a critic and Cesar, the publisher himself, with his bushy eyebrows and crystalline eyes. My miniature friend was downing oyster martinis and flipping through a copy of his novel in front of the crowd. Why am I not up there? I thought. When I saw the master of parties sitting in the third row, with his legs crossed in a pair of beige corduroys, my ego took another hit. He must be a Chicago grad by now, and dating Chloé.

From the stage Cesar was smoking a Gitane and chatting about the deranged plot of the novel (which was described as a cross between *Lolita* and *The Lord of the Rings*): As a young man, the Maestro finds in a dusty library in Genoa an old manuscript telling the most amazing story of a woman whose nipples sing when she makes love. After this life-changing discovery, the young Maestro decides to leave everything behind— mom, dad, and his job as an editor—and begins the quest to find the Venus with the Singing Nipples.

After the book presentation, we all lined up, waiting for a signed copy. Even the seagulls, who flew by brushing the fat tower of the abbey, seemed to want signed copies. As I joined the line, a cherry-red, knee-length skirt brightened my thoughts. So she's here too? I felt a tightening in my throat. Sure enough, there she was a few steps ahead, walking in line toward the podium, her hair tied back in a ponytail like a schoolgirl. The last time I'd seen her was the night at Don Otto's bakery, which now seemed a distant memory. What do I say to her? I anxiously ran through my options. And how do I greet her, a kiss on the cheek and pretend we're friends? I was not prepared to meet her. Or kiss her on the mouth? When I was insecure, I sometimes considered stupid bold moves. She was the one to kiss me first... With each step forward, the cherry-red skirt grew closer. Okay, but that was a year ago. Luckily she reached the podium a second before I did. She handed her copy of the book to Sachin.

"To Chloé, who's graduated from the best master's program...," said Sachin, signing her copy and reading aloud from the inscription. Then he went on to sign the other copies. "To Franz, the master of parties, and now also a Chicago boy..." "To Federico, a future great painter..." Then he took my copy and looked at me with an empty smile. "And what do I write for you?"

re you sure you'd like another oyster martini?"
are the last words the Indian engineer/tour
guide/chauffeur/street peddler/novelist remembers
distinctively from that entire evening.

"Yeah," he drawled, stepping down from the podium
onto the abbey's granite terrace, already visibly intoxi-
cated. "Another oyster martini."

"I'm Anna," said the woman standing in front of
him. She could have been in her forties, but there was
something extraordinarily fresh in the polite smile
beneath her big raven eyes.

"Anna with the singing nipples?" said Sachin,
winking.

"No, I'm Anna Carlevaro, the president of the
Awards," said the woman, shaking his hand in a
friendly way.

A dinner followed the book signing. Every table
was dedicated to a great novel, and on each plate was
a place card in black ink. I started searching for my
seat, looking at the plates, but I couldn't find my name.
What do I do? I still had not gone up to her.

"Here!" said a woman in her seventies, tapping on
the empty seat next to hers. She pointed to me. "Yes,
you…"

Miranda was the head of the press office at Cesar
Publishing. Although she had occupied that position

for twenty years, every writer was like the first one for her. No one was better at blackmailing a newspaper. Nobody knew how to threaten a tax audit to get a favorable review for one of her writers, or how to bribe a judge for a vote at a literary award, as she did. Her face, hidden by a waterfall of lilac veils attached to her seventeenth-century Venetian hat, contrasted with her threshing-machine voice. She was so passionate about her job that, as a writer, you'd feel you were writing just for her.

As I took my place next to Miranda at the table, named after a famous novel I'd never read, an editor from a competing publishing house was already seated. He kept adjusting his flashy yellow tie. We were still waiting for Sachin and Cesar, the publisher. Votes were being bought and sold with the same easiness as the sign of peace is exchanged in church. This award was not always won on merit.

"Are you not a member of the jury?" asked Miranda, lighting a Lucky Strike.

"Yes, I am," I said.

In fact, after my father had sold our family title, what remained of our glorious past was to be one of the Book Awards' twelve hundred jurors.

She looked at me sideways. "You know, Cesar is waiting for your manuscript."

"How did he hear about it? Did Sachin tell him?"

I could have asked her twenty more questions. "Is he really waiting for it?"

"Yes, but for how much longer?" asked Miranda calmly, taking a second puff.

I slipped my vote into her bag. "Do you have many votes?"

"Forty, with yours. If Sachin doesn't grab the Awards president's ass, we may end up in the top five."

"Which would be the first time for your publishing house," I said.

"Which would be the first time," repeated Miranda, stubbing out her Lucky Strike after the third drag.

When Sachin and Cesar joined the table, however, each holding an oyster martini, her smile vanished.

"Cesar!" she shouted. "Please tell Sachin not to grab the Awards president's ass."

"Stop grabbing her ass," said the publisher, reprimanding his author. "Sleep with her!"

"You too, Cesar, please."

From the other side of the table came a question from the competing editor with his flashy yellow tie. "So, Sachin, what are you writing now?"

Even though the tension for the upcoming awards was mounting, or maybe because it was, the chatter during dinner was casual and disjointed. Miranda asked me to send her my book. *Miranda asked me to send her my book*. I repeated it to myself over and over.

The fact that this was likely an empty invitation and prompted solely to get my vote (I would have voted for Sachin anyway) didn't bother me at all. The first part needed a rewrite in the third person, and the third part needed a rewrite in the first person—these were my sole concerns. Just by sitting next to Miranda, I felt I could run home and finish my book that same night.

Every so often, someone would look up nervously at the Awards president's table, where Anna Carlevaro had begun stuffing ballots into the precious box.

Over dessert, at the far end of the terrace, the orchestra's violas gave me an additional boost of confidence. Could it really be? "The Waltz of the Flowers"? It was. I recognized the dry and luminous beginning—a favorite waltz from my misspent youth. Whenever it was playing, I knew just what to say to a girl. I summoned my courage and crossed the glittering ballroom and walked to the table where she was sitting. I felt that all of the 450 guests of the Awards were looking at me.

"Would you like to dance?" I asked.

Chloé smiled but did not stand up. "No, thanks."

After dinner, the publishers again went out onto the medieval terrace together with their respective writers for a last chat. The sky was now overcast, but the clouds did not look aggressive—only soft and blue. Holding Sachin up by the arm, Cesar seemed to be searching the sea for omens for the coming day's verdict. I walked behind them, gathering the crumbs of their glory.

"I'm sorry I misbehaved," Sachin stuttered. He was now so drunk he sometimes missed a syllable and his pronunciation was even more awkward than usual.

"You didn't misbehave. If you want to write books, you must walk on dead bodies. If you want to win a prize, you must sleep with someone—better if she's the president of the prizes."

"So I didn't misbehave," said Sachin, relieved.

"If you go with him, you're misbehaving," Cesar said, pointing to the competing editor with the flashy yellow tie.

Before going to sleep, I walked Sachin up to his room, dragging him by his shoulders, because he seemed to have lost his motor skills. I had picked up an herbal tea for him in the abbey's kitchen, but since he had drunk sixteen oyster martinis, he still managed to throw up on every statue of every saint he could find. I held him up on the steep, wooden staircase, which smelled of wet fur. Whether this was due to the centuries or to the miniature Indian's vomit, I couldn't tell.

"I must be in good form," said Sachin, as he studied his cup of herbal tea. "Can you imagine how proud the Maestro would be: Sachin Asghar from Calcutta up for the Book Awards, the same award he won!"

I nodded glumly, holding him up. When we reached the second floor, pausing in front of Francis I of Valois's portrait, Sachin seemed to feel better. He stared intensively at that fourteenth-century painting and closed his fist in front of Francis I's unkempt reddish beard for a moment; he determinedly wiped the vomit from his mouth and stamped his feet noisily. At that exact moment, the door he was hoping for at the far end of the hallway opened.

"You're not feeling well?" said the voice of a woman.

A silhouette had stepped outside, a short bathrobe wrapped above her thick knees. Through the doorframe behind her, one could glimpse into the room of a generous, messy woman. A terrycloth sash was dangling from an armchair, a bra lay on the ground, and the ballot box was open on the floor like a mouth at the dentist's. "Would you like an aspirin?"

"My heart is up for grabs," were the last words to be heard from Sachin before he disappeared inside the Awards president's bedroom.

For a moment, I lingered in the dark, empty corridor. I asked myself what I was doing there and, in general, anywhere at all. Something great and beautiful…A year had passed and I still didn't know what the Maestro meant. No novel, no beautiful emptiness, no exporting focaccia. A gust of wind extinguished both torches on the staircase. A squeak came from the wood. Another silhouette, this one standing beside the window. Could it be someone from the publishing house, or security? The ghost of the Maestro? Sometimes I felt his presence. The silhouette moved slightly, and her profile was carved by the cold emergency light. I recognized a cherry-red skirt in the dim light.

"Is Sachin okay?"

"He's in there hitting on the Awards president."

"Sorry for before, I didn't mean to be rude," she said. "I don't know how to dance. Your old pickup line would have been better."

"My old pickup line?" I asked, confused.

"A slice of focaccia," said Chloé smiling.

She bowed her head. The black caress of her hair brushed against her cheeks. I thought of all the incredible things she had done during this year, while I had done nothing.

"And what about Franz?"

"What about him? He won't make a move," she said. "Maybe he doesn't like me."

I was the one to kiss her this time, and she didn't turn her head away. I felt her lips opening slowly. I felt the tip of her tongue. Again, she was darting it fast, like a year ago, like a girl kissing for the first time. No, she didn't belong to Franz, I liked to think. This time she didn't taste of focaccia, but of the candied fruits of the Genovese panettone which had been served for dessert. Again, I felt as if I was walking into the cold sea up to my navel, and everything seemed possible.

"See, what I don't like about you...," she said, placing both of her arms around my neck, and looking at me in the eyes, "is that you're spoiled. You study, but you don't study. You write, but you don't write. You and Franz grew up together, but he's not spoiled, and you are."

"Why don't you know how to dance?" I asked, slipping my hand inside her cherry-red skirt.

"If you come to visit in America, you can teach me," said Chloé smiling, gently taking my hand out.

The next day, as Sachin stepped out on the terrace, the vote counting was halfway through. The final race was on. In the fresh sun, and with the tension mounting, he didn't even feel a headache from the night before. Don Otto was down below, serving thin strips of focaccia with sage, and the people wistfully watched the yachts entering Portofino. The few who were chatting were distracted and couldn't keep themselves from counting votes in their heads. Typically there were no surprises and only the usual suspects would make it into the top five. But this year the fifth place was a wild card. Everyone's focus was on the favored Francesco Nero's *Two* and the underdog, the foreigner, Sachin Asghar's *The Venus with the Singing Nipples*.

The voice of the vote counter, opening up the ballots, was like a constant drumbeat.

"Nero, Pellegrini, Nero, Asghar...," called out the vote counter.

"Don't be nervous, Miranda. You'll make it to the top five," I said, fantasizing about the day my novel too would compete for the Book Awards. Chloé's kiss had fueled my imagination. "They've promised you forty votes."

"For sixteen years they've promised me forty votes," said Miranda.

Now twenty votes were left to be counted. Francesco Nero's *Two* and Sachin Asghar's *The Venus with the Singing Nipples* were neck and neck for fifth place.

Would Cesar Publishing win? Would it make it for the first time into the top five of the Book Awards? While Miranda brushed her cheeks with face powder, Cesar smoked, pacing back and forth like a man waiting to know if he's become a father.

"Relax, we're still fifth," repeated the editor with the yellow tie, placating his writer.

"But how can you count the votes, it's awful!" said the writer.

"I know," said the editor.

"Nero, Asghar, Nero, Asghar...," called out the vote counter.

Now a great, full silence descended on the terrace.

"Asghar, Nero, Asghar..."

Then, all of a sudden, one shout shot up to the sky and a hundred voices rose all around us. The engineer/tour guide/chauffeur/street peddler/novelist felt two arms around him and the smell of face powder and Lucky Strikes. He had made the top five.

Dimitri Buvlovski, Wall Street Lawyer

CHLOÉ VERDI

May 4, 2009, New York City

In September 2008 you joined Wall Street giant Sinclair, La Touche & Buvlovski. Exactly what type of tasks did they give you there, Ms. Verdi, before you were put in charge of Rosso's business?"

CHLOÉ VERDI

January 14–15, 2008, New York City

as I really sitting on the forty-second floor of the Met Life Building? I gazed down at the people walking across Park Avenue. Yes, here I am, even if it's only to take notes, and for however long it lasts.

I looked around like someone opening the door of a plane onto a landscape never seen before: Dimitri Buvlovski sitting at the conference room table in front of a cup of tea and a cup of coffee; Patrick Sinclair, another founding partner of the firm, playing with the teeth of his pocket comb; and the attorney, representing the other party, enjoying the view. From where we sat, the problems of the world seemed as small as the people on Park Avenue below.

"No, this no means no," I wrote on my notepad, transcribing the response from opposing counsel. The attorneys were negotiating a shareholders' agreement for a big retail company.

"With too many nos you go nowhere," said Sinclair.

"And with a shotgun, a no can become a yes," said Dimitri Buvlovski.

A "shotgun" or "Russian roulette" was a provision in a shareholders' agreement allowing control of the company to be transferred in a casino fashion: one party would offer a set price to buy the other party's shares and the other had no choice but to sell, or to buy out the first party at that same price. It obviously favored the richer guy, not the competent one, and therefore not the company. If a shareholder was struggling, the other party could buy him out for a dime, betting that he would have no choice but to accept.

"Are you gambling away the future of the company?" asked opposing counsel, concerned.

"We have a no-action letter from the SEC," said Buvlovski, throwing a document across the table.

"You have God on your side?"

Apparently the Russian had his casino-based strategy blessed by the Securities and Exchange Commission. A no-action letter is a request for advice to the SEC when the legality of a transaction is uncertain; if granted, the SEC takes no legal action. The problem was that law firms were flooding the SEC with requests that appeared perfectly legitimate on their face, banking on the odds that the commission would not have enough people on staff to verify the actual transaction.

There was a moment of silence in the conference room. It was difficult to negotiate with Buvlovski. He knew the law, he drank tea and coffee at the same time, and people said he gave in only to his mother.

"And we have a suite at Madison Square Garden tonight," Patrick Sinclair whispered when opposing counsel excused himself to go to the restroom. He excitedly presented a concert pass to Buvlovski. Although Sinclair was a founding partner of the firm, he showed absolutely no interest in the law. "You're coming to see her?"

"Who is she?"

"Only the World's Biggest Rock Star. She's what you are, but in the music biz!"

"We've done only two IPOs this year," said Buvlovski.

"Dimitri, nobody this year has done more than two IPOs." Sinclair shrugged his shoulders as if trying to shake off his colleague's high standards.

Buvlovski replied calmly, "Suites at Madison Square Garden, five chefs in our cafeteria, twenty limo drivers outside playing cards, first-year associate with nothing to do bumped at $165K per year...who the hell is paying for all of this crap?"

"We need to keep up with what other firms are doing," said Sinclair.

"It's a race to the bottom."

As the gray January sun began setting on the forty-two lobbies of Sinclair, La Touche & Buvlovksi, I ran after Buvlovski, who was distributing the work. He would draft the contract himself and would give something pointless to a couple of first-year associates like me. He believed that the newly hired were completely useless because law school didn't teach anything useful workwise. "Instead of paying your law school tuition," he had once told a first-year, "you should have used the money to work on your lottery strategy."

I knew that I had been hired at the last minute, end of August, only because of rules on diversity. That year there were too few women in the firm. And I knew that in July I would have to leave my spot to the newly hired.

Unless... I continued daydreaming while running after the Russian in my newly purchased Amaranth pink suit. On each floor I took it all in: the sweet smell from the gargantuan bouquets of white gardenias, the austere pictures of the partners on the walls (their smiles as tight as if they had been chewing on herring), and, quite shockingly, the shoe shiners who rubbed the attorneys' black wingtips until they shone like sapphires.

Buvlovski suddenly stopped and turned around. "Why are you following me, Ms. Chloé Ombra Allegra Verdi?"

He always insisted on calling me by my full name, which I didn't particularly like; my mother addressed me that way when she was mad at me. Instead, the general rule in the office was to go by first name, except for Buvlovski, who asked to be called by his last name.

"Is there anything else I can do, Mr. Buvlovski?"

He grunted and gestured and as I followed him down to the library, he grew increasingly agitated. The firm's library was organized on two floors; you needed a map to find your way around it. Buvlovski started pulling books from their shelves, dropping them on the floor and kicking them around in the corridor.

"Finally, here it is! This was not in the right section!" he yelled, holding the treaty he was looking for, *Privatization & Directo*. He threw a blue booklet at me. "Check everything."

I opened the booklet. It was the library's index, which listed over fifteen thousand works.

"What do you mean?" I asked.

"Please make sure that every book is in its right place by tomorrow morning."

A little past midnight, when like a girl in a fairy tale I was struggling through my completely overwhelming yet useless task, Buvlovski left the building. As I had learned from one of the other associates who every dawn delivered hundreds of pages of photocopies to his home, this is what the senior partner did every night.

He would leave his office past midnight, to check that the cleaning services would start at 12:15 on the dot and that the florist would replace only the white gardenias in the lobby (and not the rest of the flower decorations). Without asking for a car, he would walk out to Lexington Avenue, sinisterly glaring at the firm's drivers, who were playing cards on the shiny hoods of the limousines, and he would head to the Times Square–Forty-second Street subway station. If it had been up to him, none of that bullshit of limousines and white gardenias would be there. Although he was SL&B's rainmaker, he had been outvoted on any policy that had to do with "appearances." He was the firm's brain, not its looks.

After a fifty-five-minute subway ride, he would get off at the last stop of the Q line. Out there, in the cold Coney Island air, everything was dark and empty, as if the train hadn't stopped an hour outside of Manhattan but somewhere deep in old Russia. Low, anonymous storefronts, which once hosted freak shows and were now selling household appliances; a wooden roller coaster, which had already collapsed twice, curving above the ocean... You were wrong if you thought that the most overpaid lawyer, after work, would walk to his townhouse off Park Avenue.

"Dimitri, Dimitri...," a voice would call from inside the house.

And Buvlovski would push open the heavy front door of his home and walk on the worn rugs. The streetlamps' light filtered onto the Jugenstil vases and the cracked profile of a Byzantine Madonna, and onto a golden ostensory. Every night you could hear the echo of the same polonaise.

In the large, candle-lit living room an old woman was sitting at a piano. She was 102 years old and wore a long organza dress. Some people argued that she was demented, some that she was an eccentric, others said that she was living in Tolstoy's books, which she had been rereading every day since the age of nine after her parents left Russia in 1915. Her shoulder-length white wig always looked perfectly coiffed and luminous.

When he walked in, she would say, "Finally, Dimitri, I've been waiting all day." And she'd ask him to sit next to her at the piano and play the polonaise *à quatre mains*, as a duet. Sometimes she would bend over an old gramophone to play a rendition of the Kreutzer Sonata (because it had inspired a novella by Tolstoy). Then they would start to dance. The woman clung to him, she yielded, and then, despite her old age, again picked up the tempo without missing a beat. Her steps were so light and precise they seemed to lead, mocking his stiff ones.

"A polka?" she asked sometimes at the end of the first dance.

"I haven't had dinner yet, Mama," said Buvlovski.

"Dimitri," she would invariably answer in a firm but loving way. "If you are hungry, you have to come home on time. You know that dinner is at seven-thirty."

I went to the cafeteria around noon the next day. The librarian had not showed up yet. I had been working nonstop. Although it was January 15, the day was mild. The cafeteria windows were open and the other associates were lingering with their trays in the squares of sunlight. Looking over the buffets with Greek Cypriot cuisine, the honey torcetti from Lanzo, and the waiters in striped uniforms, I found it hard to believe that this was a law firm cafeteria.

Adhering to the rules of "business casual" attire, no one except for the partners wore a jacket and tie. The men, in sports shirts, and the women, in knee-length skirts, seemed all to have stepped from the cover of *Vanity Fair*. In fact, among female graduates with similar grades, SL&B would hire only the good-looking ones. The most hardworking guy in the whole building seemed to be the boy who was cleaning out the rooftop swimming pool. Law firms that looked like country clubs, lawyers who looked like models, first-year associates like me who were being compensated $165,000 a year to rearrange the books in the library...Buvlovski was right, who was paying for all of this?

"Two slices of swordfish, please," Franz said, raising his hand.

His arm—wrapped in a close-fitting, tailor-made poplin sleeve—immediately attracted the chef's attention. Franz wore a gray gabardine suit, deviating from the business casual rule, to look more senior. Who would have guessed that he had been the master of parties? That a ball without him at dawn was a failed ball? Now, in his jacket and tie, he could easily be mistaken for a junior partner.

"I should have eaten at my desk," he said, nervously checking his Blackberry, which was blinking on his tray.

"Relax," I said, aiming for his upper lip.

The chef gently laid the serving of swordfish on tinfoil.

"You kiss me, here in line, in front of everybody?" Franz whispered blushing. He had been caught off guard.

"Yes, what else are lines for?" I said, kissing him again. "You taught me that."

My spontaneity seemed to shock the entire cafeteria. Dimitri Buvlovksi, who was reviewing a document by the elevator, slowly turned his large square head and looked back at us.

Our first kiss had been kind of awkward too (standing in line, to be exact). I assume that's always the case between two friends who, at some point, cross boundaries, but in this case it was more than that. It was about passing customs. It happened on September 8, at around 5:43 p.m., at JFK. We had flown back to New York after Sachin's award, and my H-1B visa (sponsored by SL&B) was questioned at immigration. "You don't look like a lawyer," said Officer José Gonzales curtly, checking my fingerprints. Immigration officers have some power of life and death over people hoping to enter the United States. Franz showed his H-1B visa to the officer. "Yes, Ms. Verdi has been hired by Sinclair, La Touche & Buvlovski in my same department," he said. The sergeant slightly frowned with his reddish eyebrows. "You hear so many stories... How can you prove you know her, sir?" he asked. In response, the master of parties kissed me. "Next! Please move on!" said the officer, annoyed as Franz wouldn't stop kissing me.

And we have been going out ever since. I received the offer from SL&B a week before my starting date and had no time to look for an apartment, so Franz asked me if I wanted to stay at his place in Brooklyn Heights.

The first five months went by like one big holiday (unless assigned crazy useless tasks). The weekend usually began on Monday, if Franz finished early.

We'd go eat mozzarella sandwiches at JG Melon's and gossip about the office, fantasizing about what we'd do as grown-ups. On Tuesdays he was typically busy and I went by myself to the movies, and on Thursdays to a Broadway show, or vice versa. Fridays the real weekend started with a bunch of (thank God) nonlawyer friends (writers, indie producers) at El Faro downtown in front of a pitcher of sangria with fat slices of peach inside. Because I wasn't used to drinking I would eat the peach slices until I became fun to talk to.

On Saturdays we usually spent the day together in Astoria, Queens. We went shopping for the week at Titan's and bought olives in large plastic containers (much cheaper than in Manhattan). In the evenings we had dinner at Uncle George's and, after the baklava, we danced with some fishermen between the Greek flag by the entrance and the map of Rhodes posted on the toilet door. Or we went back to Manhattan and crashed the parties of the super-rich on Fifth Avenue, where there were more Picassos on the walls than guests. The master of parties always knew his way in. So I was joining him, and even learning how to dance.

It was beautiful to go home at dawn and make love while watching the skyscrapers change color. It was beautiful to do what I had never done before, and to do it with Franz, someone I now felt so close to, although so different from: he did everything well.

While Franz headed toward the elevator with his tray—he would eat in front of his computer while preparing an S-4 merger filing—I returned to the library. I picked up where I'd left off before lunch, though I was uninspired. My social life had been taking off, not my work. Ever since joining SL&B I studied the Securities Act of 1934 and attended all the seminars in the firm, but I had yet to do anything useful. My assignments varied from reorganizing folders to rearranging the library. Had I graduated in chemistry instead of law, it would have been exactly the same thing.

"Anyway, it's not a good year, Bob: we've done only two IPOs...One second...Hey, Ms. Chloé Ombra Allegra Verdi, you don't knock on doors?" said Buvlovski, trailing off as I walked inside his office.

The senior partner had not eaten his lunch yet, and his tray stood on his desk. He had already cut his swordfish into three pieces—apparently he planned to swallow the fish in three bites. Did the Russian have teeth in his stomach? Next to the tray was a document with Buvlovski's comments. His handwriting was round and neat, almost childlike. Anyone who didn't know that it was a merger agreement between two steel giants would have assumed it was a first grader's notebook.

"What do you want?" Buvlovski asked, inspecting his horrible tie, which dangled from his neck like a cow's tongue. "Did you finish your job in the library?"

"I did."

"By the way, is it the firm's policy to kiss in the cafeteria? Are we not keeping you busy?"

That's what I was hoping to hear.

"There should be...," said Buvlovski.

"Yes?" I said, holding my breath.

"...the firm's soccer tournament at Chelsea Piers to organize."

Gino's and the Waiter

CHLOÉ VERDI

May 4, 2009, New York City

Did Rosso Fiorentino go back to New York to start a company or to follow you, Ms. Verdi?" As the prosecutor detected a smile on my face he added, "Should I remind you that he's facing 137 years in jail?"

ROSSO FIORENTINO

January 2, 2008, New York City

I do have a damn room!" said Uncle Spiro with the same hostility as if I had told him he was homeless; I was only asking him if he had a vacancy in his hostel. "Sixty dollars a night."

It was my first morning in New York since January 1989 and the cold burned my face like stinging nettles. Everything looked quite the same way I had left it. Bicycles were ridden on the wrong side of the road, taxis continued to ignore ambulance sirens just as they did back then, and the client was always wrong. The key difference since the late eighties—I was told by the bus driver from the airport who was somehow alarmed—was that the ratio of single girls per guy had dropped from 7.3 to 7.2.

My bank account had also dropped, to $235. I had used my last chunk of euros to buy the plane ticket from Milan to JFK. I needed to find investors for my company. I needed to make cash, fast.

I followed Uncle Spiro to the back of his courtyard in Queens, and behind an iron door I found my assigned room. It contained a sink, a mirror, and a couple of bunk beds where some old Greek men were snoring loudly.

"Sixty dollars for this?" I asked.

"It's no longer 1989, dude."

Over the next couple of days I followed Uncle Spiro's advice. According to him, the gold rush started in a restaurant. "You have better chances to find an angel investor at Le Cirque than at Citibank," he said. I therefore applied to all of the French places on the East Side, from Le Chat Noir to Le Bilbouquet, including Le Cirque, to all of the steak houses, Morton's, Bobby Van's, and Smith & Wollensky. I researched in detail every restaurant I applied for, but nobody seemed to be hiring. The response was always the same: "We're staffed."

One day I showed up at the hottest spot of the moment: Madiba in Brooklyn. It served good South African food and mojitos with fresh mint. A large yellow poster of Nelson Mandela welcomed you at the entrance. The restaurant was so popular that you had to book a month in advance to get a table. After carefully reviewing my résumé, where I had listed that I was just two exams short of graduating from university, the manager said, "I'm sorry, you're overqualified."

t seven on the clear morning of January 10, I showed up at Gino's, on Sixtieth and Lexington, my last Italian before going Asian. I waited approximately an hour in front of a shutter bolted by a lock until Michael, the restaurant's cashier, showed up.

"Twenty percent of Harvard Business School graduates are without jobs. Don't take it personally," said Michael as he opened the lock after a couple of tries. "Where are you from?"

"New York," I said.

I followed the cashier inside. He switched on the restaurant's lights.

As the lights came on, I was flashed by a herd of zebras, chased by arrows, running on flamboyant red wallpaper.

"Good, you don't have a visa problem," said Michael. Then he turned to the old man who had just walked in and pointed at me with his chin: "He's asking if we can use him... Bruno called in sick. We're missing a waiter."

Gino's was a true Italian-American restaurant. It had the most eccentric wallpaper and served the heaviest tortellini with cream in town.

"We don't need anybody," said the old man, who was also Gino, the owner. "I don't care if Bruno is sick. Eight waiters can do the job of nine. I've always worked for one and a half."

"Lucien Verger has booked for tonight," said Michael.

"Verger booked," Gino said, pondering. Immediately the name of Lucien Verger acquired a biblical stature in my imagination. Who could it be? What kind of big shot if they need one waiter just for him? Gino pointed to the wallpaper, testing me. "Do you know why the zebras are missing a stripe?"

I nodded. As part of my in-depth restaurant research, I had read several *New York Times* articles on that wallpaper. "In 1947 the designer messed up the design and it was too expensive to redo it," I said.

"Yes." Gino smiled. "It became famous by mistake, like the leaning Tower of Pisa. Do you remember in which movies it's featured?"

As the articles pointed out, over the years that wallpaper had become a bit of an obsession for him.

"I do," I said. "Woody Allen's *Mighty Aphrodite* and *The Royal Tenenbaums*."

Gino nodded. "You seem awfully in the know," he said, squinting. "Are you here to spy so you can open a restaurant like mine?"

"No, being a waiter is just a starting point," I reassured him smiling. "I want to conquer a girl. I want to make lots of money."

"Well, that's not going to happen here," said Gino, smiling back at me. Then he looked at Michael. "Let's give him a shot for one night."

Since I had a couple of hours before starting my first paid job, I decided to go and see where she lived. I pulled out the address I had gotten from the secretary of the University of Chicago. I had written it on a wrinkled paper napkin, which to me felt more important than the Magna Carta.

It was a cold, electric day. There was that mineral smell in the air of when it's about to snow. I tried not to smile as I walked past my reflection in the windows of Bloomingdale's, and for no reason I felt like waving to the hot dog vendors. I wanted to jump up and down as if I had just been offered a job at JP Morgan.

I got off the subway at Borough Hall and, after checking the address three or four times, I sat on a bench.

"Here I am!" I shouted, answering to the last words Chloé had said to me in Italy. "I'm here to teach you how to dance." Across the river the sun had just come out from behind the clouds and lit Lower Manhattan, and the skyscrapers were glittering like inaccessible sanctuaries. You're there now? I thought with a shiver. You did go places.

To fuel myself I had a couple of glorious daydreams while gazing at the skyline. I was good at that. I could already hear my admirers praise me as if I were Mick Jagger: "His best move? Not finishing school." I could hear my enemies saying what studio chief Jack Warner had said about Reagan when he was elected president: "It's our fault, we should have given him better parts."

Then I checked the address on the paper napkin for the fifth time and looked at the door just a couple of steps away. It had just been repainted blue. Tonight you'll walk in there, I thought. I felt a match light in my stomach.

When I showed up at Gino's it was five in the afternoon and already dark outside. The temperature was dropping and on the pavement a glaze of frost was beginning to sparkle. Michael gave me a worn cotton jacket and a couple of tips on how to clear tables.

Gino's was a good place to start waiting. You learned the ingredients of the Secret Sauce and met loads of people, from downtown literary agents to some Democratic Party financiers to all of the city's bums. Every night they stood in front of Gino's waiting for the garbage. I had already become friends with one of them, "Martin, the bum-economist," as he had introduced himself, claiming an expertise in finance.

Young waiters like me took orders, took business cards, and wondered when the gold rush would start.

My gold rush didn't start too badly that evening. The first customer was a lady from Jersey dining before going to the opera. At first I thought her stingy, as she used the libretto for *Turandot* to line up each dish on the menu with its price. But she left me a 25 percent tip. Then two Broadway actors sat down placidly, like horses in the sun.

"So what do you recommend as an appetizer?" asked one of the two actors, looking at me. "No, no, I'm allergic to seafood. And what about a steak tartar, with no egg, cooked and not raw, and a lighter meat instead of beef like chicken?"

Sometimes taking orders was a way of getting to know people. At other times it was a complicated process. I wrote something down, crossed it out, wrote it down again, and now and then I was distracted, remembering what was about to happen, in just a few hours, and across that low tide, in the distance, I thought I could see two green fires. Even though the Maestro had taught me how, that night it was really tough to wait.

"And are the artichokes tender?"

"They're so tender," I said, smiling.

Toward nine-thirty, a new customer came in. A sudden calm descended on the chaos of Gino's, like a whaler entering port. Behind the bar, Angelo raised his eyes from the bottle of dolcetto he was decanting, and Michael smoothed the gray sideburns at his temples. This must be Lucien Verger, I thought. His solemnity was emphasized by the fact that no one dared to approach him as he stood by the PLEASE WAIT HERE TO BE SEATED sign.

He sported a round, perfumed figure and was dressed in layers like an onion. Over his navy-blue suit he was wearing a green MIG-20 bomber jacket. Here was my angel investor. I was standing there in front of his table with my notepad open, in front of my benefactor, to whom I owed my first paid job. You don't get a second chance to make a good first impression, I said to myself.

"Tell me, kid, can you put down your notepad and look at me?" said Lucien Verger, losing interest for a moment in the menu. "Right, look at me carefully." He smiled. "Tell me, do I look like an ogre?"

"What do you mean?" I asked, surprised.

Verger took off his glasses, his egg-white nose sticking out over his cheeks even farther. Although he claimed to be French, everyone said he was Greek. The long red hair, which grew beneath his completely bald crown, moved a touch as a waiter passed by too closely.

"You know what I mean. Do I look like an ogre?"

"You look more like an angel to me," I said, smiling.

"Then why will no one ever come out to seat me in this restaurant!" he said, pointing at me in a fit of rage.

I decided to answer the question with a question. "Perhaps because people become a little shy around someone as important as you are?" I suggested smiling.

"No, because I am a fucking ogre!"

So I've ended up with a masochist angel investor, I thought. You never win.

Around eleven that evening, Michael closed the door from the inside as the waiters were setting up tables with clean linen for the next day. Gino started to count the cash; the restaurant didn't accept credit cards. On Thursday nights you could find more money in Gino's cash register than if you robbed the ATM machine on Sixty-second and Lex.

"You're going to see the girl now?" asked Gino as he sipped coffee and looked inside the cup.

I felt another match lighting in my stomach.

"You know it's dropping into the teens tonight," he added.

"They said it's going to be the coldest night of the year," confirmed Michael. "People are staying home."

"Thanks, kid," said Verger, leaving. Then he wrapped some dollar bills around his business card. Since he thought he didn't have friends, he gave his card to everyone he met. The loneliness of successful people, I thought. He smiled. "If it doesn't work out with the girl, give me a ring. I have plenty!"

When I emerged from the subway, a thick layer of light blue frost already glazed the street. I sat down on the same bench, in front of her house, where I had been sitting that morning. The temperature continued to drop. I looked up and noticed that her window on the second floor was still dark. She must still be at work. The wind from the upper bay was stronger and icy but I couldn't feel it.

Every car that turned the corner, every passerby, every nothing...it could be her.

Snow White,
the Porn Star

CHLOÉ VERDI

May 4, 2009, New York City

The prosecutor shook his head in disbelief. "Porn? Really?"

ROSSO FIORENTINO

I told you it wasn't going to work," said Lucien Verger in his Franco-Greek English as I felt two arms hoisting me up off of the sidewalk and dragging me somewhere inside.

When I opened my eyes, a 3,000-watt lamp blinded me. Was I in an operating suite? I tried to clutch at something. A short guy named Rex was calling out, "Snow White, Behind the Scenes Part I!" and someone crouched between a girl's legs was throwing away the third razor. Where the hell was I? Lucien Verger paraded in front of me in a white bathrobe, his hairy red knees sticking out. I slowly remembered that I had dragged myself to the address listed on his business card.

"You know what my great-uncle always said?" said Verger, sitting on the couch where I was lying. "Beat your woman every night. And if you don't know why, she will."

As he untied my shoes, I realized that I couldn't feel anything from my waist down. I was frostbitten.

He then rubbed another finger of rum on my lips to get my circulation going.

"And you've been too good to her," said Verger. "Especially if she's an ex-junkie."

"But Chloé doesn't—" I gave a sudden, hard cough.

"You told me that. She's unstable, her arms are like Swiss cheese, and she doesn't drink. Ex-junkie, big time...But check out all the sexy chicks here!"

"And you're a sexy boy," said a sweet voice. Two nails, which looked slightly bitten notwithstanding the nail polish, caressed my face. "My name is April."

I continued to look around more and more confused, wondering where I could possibly be. Rex, the director, called again, "Quiet on set, camera rolling,...action!" With those magic words an almost total silence descended over the room. You could only hear the *bip bip* of the digital camera. The girls were lined up against a wall, well coiffed and with bright gloss on their lips, and they said things that made no sense like "I was in seventy films last year," or "I'm always faithful to my boyfriend except when I'm in bed." Since she had called me "sexy boy," I realized I was waiting to hear what April had to say.

"It's my first girl-girl scene," said April, smiling, sounding both shy and proud. "Since I was fifteen my dream has been to work with Marie Alice." While the camera followed her, she again caressed my cheek with two fingers. "But I still like sexy boys!"

Finally, with a slow pan the camera moved in on Marie Alice, who was completely naked. She had tawny red hair and her beauty spots were scattered on her clear shoulders like a handful of pepper.

"Maybe you know everything about me," she said, spreading her legs and revealing her pubis, which was as bare as a peeled apple. "But did you know that I was born in Moscow on Valentine's Day?"

"Cut! Okay, girls!" said Rex, applauding briefly. "Please, Marie Alice...You've been a bit under par lately."

"Please, M.A.," said Verger.

"But what's this?" I said, holding my head with both hands. "Weren't you supposed to be a big shot, a tycoon, an angel investor? You produce porn?"

"Porn fairy tales," specified Verger sorrowfully. "Mainstream porn is no longer selling. Internet and YouPorn are killing us."

To the soft, eighties tones of "I Like Chopin," a gaffer pushed a coat rack with the film's costumes into the room. The costumes seemed even more deranged than the girls' lines. There was the Walt Disney blue tulle dress for Snow White, and the dwarfs' clogs, pointy hats, and matching outfits.

I tried to move my toes, which were still stuck together inside my socks. "I Like Chopin" went the song again. That had been my first slow dance. But I didn't think of my first love, Kerry, with whom I had danced to it, or of Marinella. I thought of her, and what had happened earlier that night.

Taxi after taxi, car after car, had stopped in front of the same spot where I was waiting. But it was always someone else coming out: a heavy man in his fifties, an Asian woman and her dog, a young guy carrying a guitar... Every time I could feel my pulse speed up when the taxi stopped and the door opened, and then slow down again when I realized it wasn't her. Gradually my vision became blurred. The wind was blowing harder in my face, and my eyes were watering, and the water was turning into frost on my eyelashes. I could now only see a few feet away. Sometimes a shadow would go by, until one stopped. A match lit in my stomach. Her breath was condensed in the cold air that smelled of snow. A thousand matches lit in my stomach. A taller, broader shadow was handling a pair of keys... All the matches went off at once. Why? How? What was Franz doing there? Before they could see me I ran back to the subway.

"You really want to be on film, Rosso?" said Verger. "Aren't you all frostbitten?"

"I don't know," I said.

"Of course you must be on film," April said, unbuttoning my trousers. "You're so cute!"

The magic words, "Quiet on set, camera rolling,...action," descended again over us. Marie Alice was lying on a sofa bed, in the middle of the room, in her Snow White blue tulle dress. With a bit of gel in her hair, a dusting of glitter on her cheeks, and her fresh breath that smelled of Apple Halls, she really looked like Snow White.

The male actors, on the other hand, were annoying and not at all dwarflike (except for their exceptionally large genitals). They operated in sync like a special squad. Sneezy came from behind, Dopey was on top, and the others arrived one by one. Being regular guests of Playboy TV seemed to have gone to their heads. Sometimes they jumped up and down on the sofa bed yelling. Sometimes they laughed and pointed at me while I attempted to engage in some action with Jen and April, despite my left foot being frostbitten.

"And what is that supposed to be? An orgy?" they said, mocking me. "We already have Sleepy, you know that!" Or they tried to intimidate me. "Watch your back! Better once with Snow White than seven times with the seven dwarfs!"

At around two in the morning someone cleaned off the seats of Verger's limousine and we went out to shoot the exteriors. To keep costs down everything had to be shot just in a few hours. The girls took a break; they had worked hard and were tired, and were all having vitamin drinks while looking at the moon. The male actors were even more tired; they seemed utterly exhausted.

After we all got in, the car merged onto Third Avenue. Outside the temperature was rising and wet snow was falling on the street.

"Rosso, are you up for the next scene?" asked Rex, the director, giving a dirty look to the male actors who sat breathless and bunched together at the back of the limousine.

I nodded.

"Thank God someone came to work today!"

"Where are you from?" April whispered in my ear.

"Italy," I said, instead of New York.

"Wow, Italy. Is that what makes you so good?"

"Now, let's not get arrogant, Rosso," Rex cautioned me. "Let's keep our eyes on the stars and our feet on the ground."

The limousine curved gently over the wet snow and the camera again began doing its *bip bip* sound, but Marie Alice was exhausted. Her eyes were big and anxious, and the silver sparkles glittered quietly on her cheeks.

"You can't even fake an orgasm anymore, M.A.," said Verger shaking his head, desolate.

Around four in the morning the crew took us back home. Since she also lived in Queens, Marie Alice walked a stretch of the way with me. I was heading back to Uncle Spiro's.

It was snowing heavily now and a strip of white gathered on the roofs of Astoria. The air was clean. Marie Alice's mood was better, because they had given her the blue tulle dress, and she kept it slightly lifted so that it wouldn't get wet.

"You know, you really amazed me," said Marie Alice breaking the silence. "They always expect everything of us girls, but for male actors the expectations are much lower."

"Why did you quit ballet?" I asked.

Marie Alice slowed her walk to catch her breath. Her exhalations condensed in the freezing air.

"When I was a little girl my mother took me to dance class every day. Then one day she went away with a friend of my uncle and stopped taking me. Being a strip dancer paid better than being a ballerina, and films paid even better. But it wasn't only a question of money...maybe it just happened." Marie Alice dabbed at her eye makeup, which had smeared from crying. "But if I go on like this, I guess they'll fire me..." She turned around and looked back. "And why have you sunk to my level?"

I too looked back at the clear tracks we had made in the snow.

"Oh, this is nothing," I said, smiling. I felt two tears flow silently down my cheeks. "I've done so much worse."

Focaccia House:

The Start-up

CHLOÉ VERDI

May 4, 2009, New York City

The prosecutor this time could not summon the courage to face the blue magnetic flag of the State of New York, but simply murmured, "So, the first investor of the company was a porn producer?"

ROSSO FIORENTINO

January 27–29, 2008, New York City

I'd had a strange dream. I'm with a girl. I'm trying to give her pleasure, but it's not working. I try with my penis, I try with some electric toy. Nothing. She's not feeling anything. She wants me to put a foot inside her. I'm afraid of hurting her. When I put all of my head in, to my surprise I see someone else inside the girl: a policeman who's looking for his squad car. My hands are bloodied. I'm holding the electric toy that continues to vibrate. I sense the pressure of the policeman's gun against my neck. I'm waiting for my execution. I've always been waiting for it.

"Did I hurt her?" I ask.

"No, to the contrary you succeeded," says the policeman. "You gave her pleasure. I shall knight you. What is your family crest?"

I suddenly feel the relief of bad news becoming good. I was expecting to be executed but instead I'm being knighted.

"What is your family crest?" asks the policeman again.

I wipe my bloodied fingers on the electric toy. "Five burgundy stripes on a background of gold..."

Slowly, the edges of the ceiling came together. The ceiling was so close to my face I could smell the paint. In the other bunks my roommates were still snoring loudly. Outside it was snowing.

At eight o'clock that morning I went to check on the renovations at 6 Astoria Boulevard, which was around the corner from where I stayed.

"Where are the gringos?" asked Miroal Bontes, a very chatty Portuguese contractor who constantly drinks Dr Pepper. He had completed the job, following my plans, and turned a pet bird shop into a bakery. I double-checked: the brick oven was there, the counter too, and the walls had just been repainted light melon. There was a fresh smell of paint. Through the small windows I could see the curtains from the restaurant next door. Always good to have some action around.

"Where's the money?" asked the contractor again.

"I don't have it now," I said, taking the can of Dr Pepper from his hand and putting it inside my trash bag. "I'll pay you next time."

When I got off the subway at Fifty-ninth and Lexington for my second meeting, it was ten o'clock. The cold, clean air strengthened the sense of well-being I'd woken up with. The flags of the Plaza Hotel were waving in the sky high and proud, and Central Park was beautiful in the snow.

I thought again about last night's dream, funny it was about my family's crest. True, somehow different, yet I decided to take it as a good omen.

My next meeting was with Martin, the bum-economist who lived under the grating on the northeast corner of Sixty-first and Fifth. I passed FAO Schwarz to my right and stopped at the grating.

"Where are the gringos?" said Martin's rough voice from inside. It seemed that everybody was asking me the same question. To compensate him for his services, I would typically bring Martin empty cans, which he then took to Lincoln Center to turn into cash. "Not cans again!" he said.

Under the grating, from the top of an iron ladder, I caught a glimpse of his blond beard and two intensely blue eyes. The metal gate opened. I clung to the steep ladder, wrapping my trash bag of empty cans around my wrist, and climbed down. Martin's basement was not welcoming. It was empty, cold, and the floor was a carpet of gum and cigarette stubs that passersby rained down upon him.

"You've drunk one hundred Red Bulls in two weeks?" asked Martin, reluctantly taking the trash bag I was carrying. "Seven cans a day?"

"And how much dope did you smoke?"

The smell of black afghan that was rising from the grating was so strong that it dizzied even the Pierre Hotel's doorman.

"When the fuck are you going to pay me with cash?"

"This baby needs every penny right now," I said, handing him the business plan. I wiped my mouth nervously and held my breath. "I made the adjustments you recommended. Will this work, Martin?"

Martin took a long drag of hashish, until he coughed, and commenced reading the plan.

Martin was known as the bum-economist because every evening he picked a copy of the *Wall Street Journal* out of the garbage on Fifth Avenue. He was perfectly up to date twelve hours later. Martin belonged—or so he claimed—to the mythical underground society of the Mole People. The legend of a subterranean city, he told me, had started with the Freedom Tunnel— an almost three-mile stretch of underground rail line that was built in the heart of Harlem in the 1930s by a man named Robert Moses. The rail line was used as a route for freight trains until 1980, when it was discontinued due to the increased use of trucking for transportation. It was then that something happened in the dark, abandoned tunnel…a society was born, a new tent city, complete with pirated electricity and TV, organized under its own rules—no stealing, no yelling, respect for each other; governed by its own president, the Lord of the Tunnel; and populated by its own people, the Mole People. The underground city, even more efficient and dollar-intelligent, was rising beneath the actual city. Although the Freedom Tunnel was eventually abandoned in the late 1990s, the spirit of the tunnel continued, New York's gratings became connected, and the Mole People built their own communication system and economy. For every empty can Martin collected, they paid him a nickel at Lincoln Center; for a dollar, Freddy, the bum on Thirty-second, would fix his stove; George the Mole Guy, who lived under the grating next to a Food Emporium, would ship to Martin abandoned surplus mozzarella; and the pushers of Alphabet City gave him cheap hash in exchange for his views on the euro–dollar fluctuations.

I had met Martin on my first day at Gino's. I was throwing out the trash. Between sharing the dregs of Chianti Ruffino and leftover pasta in clam sauce, we had become friends.

"Do you like the competition analysis against Domino's and Pizza Hut?" I asked, excitedly.

"You have to get one thing straight in your nonsensical brain. Your competitors are not Domino's or Pizza Hut," said Martin, "but the hot dog stands on the corner. If you do better than those guys, you'll eat Domino's for breakfast."

A passerby tossed a cigarette stub through the bars, and Martin picked it up and lit it, smoothing his blond, smelly beard.

"You think it can work?" I asked again.

"I think it can," he said smiling.

At eleven o'clock I crossed the street to Central Park for my next meeting. Would they show up? I had sent a letter three weeks earlier to my good friends in Italy, telling them when and where to meet me, but I was afraid they wouldn't come. Why would they? Because I promised them 10 percent of a start-up which was worth zero? True, 10 percent of zero was still zero. But there they were.

Don Otto and Sachin were waiting for me on a bench by the entrance of the Children's Zoo, just as I had specified. The baker, as large as a cliff, was holding his flower friend on his lap and was sitting next to the miniature Indian with his voluminous hair. I walked over in the snow and shook their hands quickly without knowing what to say at first. I felt something new inside. It had been so long since someone took me seriously that I had forgotten how it felt.

"So what's the big idea?" asked Sachin eagerly, treading up and down on a patch of snow to keep warm. He looked up as if the Trump Tower was about to crash on his head. "What's the company about? And who is this Lucien Verger? Some prominent financier, a lobbyist, a benefactor, a famous French chef?"

I looked at Don Otto. He had transplanted his old flower friend that had hung above his oven in Italy into a larger pot, wrapped with foil to protect it from the cold.

"See, Primrose did want to come to America," I said, smiling.

Don Otto smiled too.

"Yeah, Don, with this fucking flower you're driving all the chicks away," complained the miniature Indian. "They think we're perverts!"

"And with your tic they think you're on acid," said Don Otto.

"What a dream team, two perverts on acid!" yelled Sachin, then he calmed down. "So, Rosso—what is it?"

We started discussing the plan as we walked through the park toward the Reservoir. We walked and interrupted each other, excitedly raising a thousand possibilities, and at times we would stop to watch a girl jog by. When we reached the Reservoir, the water was frozen, and the skyscrapers looked uncertain in the midday light, like thirty-year-olds searching for a future.

Since it was their first time in the city, Don Otto and Sachin wanted to see the sights. We continued our talk on the deck of the Staten Island ferry, among brokers, a group of ukulele players, and mothers alone with many children. Battery Park gently slipped away.

Manhattan's toothless smile seemed hungrier now. It was snowing again, but it was no longer windy and the snow fell nicely into the ocean.

It was early evening when we got to Astoria, Queens. There was a Christmas Eve atmosphere in the happiest of boroughs. The roasted chickens were revolving in Uncle George's shop window and dripping onto the potatoes underneath, and couples walked arm in arm in the cold air. Lights dotted the windows and the balcony railings, as in Rapallo during the July feast. We shopped at the Trade Fair Supermarket and, like three kooks in the snow, we dragged everything to 6 Astoria Boulevard: the heavy bags of flour, the cans of oil, the brewer's yeast (to make the dough soft but not mushy), the malt (so that the dough made love to the palate).

The place smelled as clean and fresh as I had left it that morning. Without even unpacking we got down to business at once. Don Otto mixed the dough, I washed the oven, and Sachin checked that the fans blew the air into the courtyard. Around midnight, the baker took the first pan out of the oven, the pilot pan. The white lunar craters of the cheese focaccia were crackling, waiting for us.

"It's like in Rapallo," said the little Indian, breaking the silence that had fallen over the table. "You don't think it's like in Rapallo?"

"It's like in Rapallo," I nodded, trying to convince myself. I had given up on inhaling Drakkar Noir and kept a bottle just for comfort. That night I was too tense and I took a couple of hits. Now I couldn't distinguish any flavor.

After slowly untying his apron, Don Otto shook his head and rinsed his neck. Then he put on a new shirt. "Told you, guys, it's not moist enough for the oil to get inside."

That night I slept fitfully, half awake and constantly aware of the edges of my body. Sachin instead was sleeping soundly. He was lying on a chair next to me, and every so often he moved in his sleep to change position. Don Otto wasn't there. He'd been right, of course; a tennis shoe sole would've tasted better. That night I prayed to the Christ of the Abyss, not to relax but to ask for something. I'll give you fifty cents for every dollar I make, I promised. At some point, outside, a restaurant waiter shook out a tablecloth in the snow.

"Isn't he back yet?" asked Sachin, stretching in his chair at around eight o'clock in the morning. "Maybe he's gone out to look for a woman. In my view he's not making good focaccia because he's still a virgin. It's no longer affecting only his balls."

"Damn, he could deal with his balls some other time! Verger is due here in three hours."

By the time the emerald-green limousine pulled up outside, several baking pans were cooling by the open window. After spending all night at Café Omonia, drinking coffee and listening to a Greek ballerina singing love songs, Don Otto had come back just in time to mix a little focaccia. The table was set with paper plates and a bottle of Vermentino wine.

Lucien Verger came in noisily. "It's not a takeout joint, it's not a restaurant, and it's not a pizzeria. Can someone tell me what the fuck it is?"

He removed a beaver-fur coat lined with bright velvet. When he was thinking of investing, he was always on edge and asked a lot of questions without listening to the answers.

"I want to help you out, I want you to hook up with the girl again...," said the Greek. "But who the fuck's telling me what a focaccia house is? Okay, a bakery. And what's focaccia?"

"Cheese focaccia is a slice of moon," said Sachin, raising a finger. "Plain focaccia is the thousand navels of the most beautiful women."

"Ah, you're the writer," said Lucien Verger, lowering his voice. For a second the harshness vanished from his small eyes, and the Greek grew calm. Was his secret dream to be a publisher? He frowned. "Rosso told me about you. You were short-listed for a big prize. Are you writing now?"

"I scribble," said Sachin with an empty smile. After the prize he no longer felt like a street vendor on a special mission, but like someone who had nothing else to say.

Out from behind Verger's round, scented figure stepped the slender one of Marie Alice. Since they didn't shoot on Sundays she had agreed to accompany him as a taste tester. She folded her bright raincoat over her knees and with her hand she shook some snow out of her red hair.

"You think it can work?" asked Verger.

"I don't know, the water and the air are a bit different here," said Don Otto, shrugging his shoulders.

"And why are they different?"

"The water and the air are different in Rapallo."

"But who gives a fuck about Rapallo?" said the Greek, staring intensely at the velvet collar of his beaver fur draped over his arm. "And you, are you an anticapitalist baker?"

"Me? Yes."

The cheese focaccia was served together with the plain focaccia. While Marie Alice was amused by the small mist that rose from the crust, Lucien Verger bit in cautiously, and then again, studying the flavor. I was handed a slice, but didn't dare to taste it.

"Not bad...," said Verger.

"But it's so good!" shouted Marie Alice, leaving the neat imprint of her teeth in the slice.

"Not bad," repeated Verger, rescuing a lump of cheese that had fallen onto his chin. "Try it, Rosso!"

Before leaving, Verger wanted to know everything. He examined the business plan, growing even more agitated with each new question: what were the ingredients, how many pounds on a daily average could the bakery produce, and could home delivery justify the quality/price ratio?

"You eat focaccia in the bakery," said Don Otto calmly. "You don't deliver it."

"So you really are an anticapitalist baker."

"And you are one sweet-smelling primrose!" said Marie Alice, leaning over the flowering plant above the oven. Then she put on her raincoat and turned her head and smiled.

As the emerald limousine disappeared down Astoria Boulevard, leaving clear furrows in the snow, we lingered in the road. A bit of sun was shining over the low, white houses.

"This batch was like Rapallo," said Sachin.

"Right," I smiled, taking another bite.

"Right, last night I was rushing to go out, I forgot the malt," said Don Otto, staring after the tire marks the limousine had left in its wake. "But who the hell did you pray to last night?" he asked me. "The Christ of the Abyss?"

Focaccia House Inc.

CHLOÉ VERDI

May 4, 2009, New York City

The public attorney again raised his eyes at the flag of the State of New York, at the glorious sunrise depicted therein, and sighed. "From zero to hero in the blink of an eye..." Then he began to review the company's bank statements. "Tell me, why did Rosso Fiorentino withdraw $125,000 from the checking account on April 3, 2008...in *cash*?"

ROSSO FIORENTINO

February 3–May 11, 2008, New York City

Y ou know those cold rainy days when unexpectedly, at dusk, a beautiful sun comes out? Well, the opening of Focaccia House was a bit like that.

For the first two weeks our shop on Astoria Boulevard, Queens, was completely empty. Passersby seemed not to notice it, as if they were shielded by imaginary blinders. Holding cups of black coffee and pretzels they had bought at the hot dog stands, they walked by heading straight for the subway. Martin, the bum-economist, was right: hot dog vendors were killing us.

One Wednesday afternoon a pretty girl who had been waiting for the bus walked in. She too held a pretzel wrapped up in a paper napkin. "You don't have pizza?" she asked displeased. "I work out to eat pizza."

Then, halfway into the second week, Sachin the engineer reassembled the oven exhaust so that the hot air spewed into the street and no longer into the courtyard. A sweet, warm smell permeated the sidewalk and, to use his words, the passersby started to veer toward the bakery like jellyfish swept by a current. In other words, enough people started coming in for the shop to survive that first month.

I worked from dawn into the evening. The only break I took was to go and see the sunset. I liked watching the last sun punch the masses of steel and concrete of Lower Manhattan, and to witness the moment when the office lights blinked on. The skyscrapers lit up in patches made me think of her, of the scars on her arms, of when she laughed, of how fast she moved her tongue when she kissed. Ex-junkie, big time! Verger's words came to mind.

Around seven in the evening, I would return to Queens and stand in front of the orange bakery sign Federico, the painter, had designed and sent from Italy. Although I had asked him to join us, he had sided with my father's view, that art's greatest patrons are grappa and national health care. You don't need me to come, he had written in his letter. You're the luckiest guy in town now! I would look at the sign for some time. Its amber light flashed on and off in the shop's front window.

Although during that winter the economy kept slowing down, with the GDP losing another half-point, by the end of March the bakery was finishing in the black. We each leased a Suzuki Bandit 1200, which could rev up to 170 miles an hour on the FDR

Drive, and we kept a table at the Palladium on Sundays. I had moved out of Uncle Spiro's to rent a studio on Jackson Avenue. Here I no longer heard old Greeks snoring, just a slight rattle of the N train as it went by. I had also bought Martin a 150-kilowatt generator and a 16-inch flat-screen TV with a subscription to Bloomberg, so he could be up-to-date on finance in real time.

Verger, who'd been paid back with 7 percent interest, better than the returns on his AT&T bonds, decided to invest in a second bakery.

As always, the hardest thing was to find a good baker. We looked everywhere among the brave and the hungry: from firefighters, who are famous for their food as they cooked their own meals seven days a week, to dirt-poor Bedford-Stuyvesant New Yorkers, to a list of retired boxers. But nobody could keep it up, said Don Otto.

Then one evening, outside the Palladium, we met Adam, who was fed up with being a bouncer. Adam was a proud Somalian American, with a neck as thick as a washing machine. Like Don Otto, he would knead with his left hand when his right cramped.

A manager, on the other hand, was easy to find. We posted an ad on LinkedIn and we were flooded with résumés. Out of the stack of applications that came in every week, we chose a blond Irish kid named David Jeffrey. He had studied at Dartmouth and Yale, had been fired by UBS, and was neither too stupid nor too smart to create problems.

One morning in April, Franz showed up at our bakery in Queens, where we were conducting inter-views for our second opening. He had seen our ad. He was wearing a white shirt with a dash of pink that worked well with his crow-black hair. He had a gym bag slung over his shoulder with his name and title as vice-president monogrammed on it. After his mas-ter's at the University of Chicago, he was first hired by SL&B and then was poached by HWBC. He was unstoppable.

"A slice of cheese focaccia?" said Sachin, smiling.

I cut a corner slice, the best one, where the two edges of the crust seal in the cheese. In the strong light of that spring morning, it was blatantly obvious why Chloé had chosen him and not me.

"The truth is she dumped me," Franz said, grimac-ing, as if he had read my mind. "For Andy, an architect."

"She'll dump him as well," I said.

"An onion slice too?" asked Sachin.

Franz took a few sure steps around the bakery and looked outside at the desolate street in Queens. His brown leather shoes, John Lobb Philip II, that I had seen him wear once at a party, had just been polished to a brilliant shine.

"Hey, right now you guys are the only ones mak-ing money in America! I've been checking you out," said Franz, rubbing his hands energetically. "I was wondering if you needed a co-manager, David Jeffrey must be swamped. And I could bring you a ton of customers! Your new store in Midtown is going to be right opposite my friends' offices at UBS."

Sachin lifted his eyes from Franz's résumé. He looked at him fearfully, like someone seeing a wounded hawk crash to the ground. "You've been fired too?"

The day our second bakery opened its doors, winter had returned. The weather forecast, and in particular the air pressure, always had a profound effect on me. Our new bakery was a shoebox on Sixth Avenue and Forty-fourth Street, between Duane Reade and White & Case's forty-two floors. As in Rapallo, we had a bell that rang when you opened the door.

"Why are you so pale, Primrose?" said Marie Alice, walking in, midafternoon.

She held the door half open a moment, so the doorbell that kept on ringing would get Don Otto to lift his head. She was braving the icy cold, in a pair of tight orange shorts that let her belly button triumph over her white freckled legs. Since Don Otto didn't raise his head, she stuck her hand in the dough he was stretching and scattered it around.

"Ooh, what a bore you are, always kneading!" said Marie Alice. "Are you a workaholic?"

"Long live the bakers!" said Don Otto.

"Sachin says you're always working because you're a virgin," laughed Marie Alice. "Are you a virgin?"

"Sachin's a gossip, like all writers," said Don Otto.

"He says that you're a virgin because the first time you did it, you didn't get hard and the girl started to laugh," said Marie Alice, stifling a laugh herself.

"Sachin's a piece of shit."

"Look, that happens all the time to the actors on set..."

Marie Alice spread even more of the dough out over the table. Her nail polish, an orange less intense than that of her shorts, stood out amid the wet flour.

"So is it true, Primrose, you're pale because you're jealous?" she asked.

Don Otto slowly raised his big round eyes from the dough. "Whom should Primrose be jealous of?"

A group of schoolkids had entered the store. They formed a polite semicircle in front of the cash register, each putting some coins on the counter. They might have been seven or eight years old and the girls wore blue skirts and the boys a uniform with checkered ties.

"How much is a slice?" asked Don Otto, turning to me.

"Seventy-five cents," I said, counting the coins on the counter. "We're missing a quarter."

A little girl stepped forward and put down a quarter.

"Eliza, we need that for the subway!" shouted one of the kids.

"Focaccia for everybody, move it!" said Marie Alice, taking out a few singles from the tight pockets of her orange shorts and slamming them on the counter. Then she looked at each of us, one at a time. "You should be ashamed of yourselves."

Unlike the opening in Queens, that evening was a good start, with a lot of elbowing, like when something's happening in town, like during fashion week. Around ten o'clock, people started coming out of the theater. Women were rushing in the cold, on very high heels, the men following behind putting on their overcoats, and everyone came spilling into the bakery. The bell was constantly tinkling.

Paper-wrapped packages with large oil stains were sliding nonstop across the counter, and the line outside was longer than the one in front of the Broadway shows. People were joining in simply because others were, and then were trying to figure out what to order. Plain focaccia, focaccia with onions, sage focaccia? It was a new language for midtown Manhattan. Adam's and Don Otto's arms were dripping like meat cooking on spits.

When the crowd from the evening shows ended and we were ready to close, the bell on the door rang again. It was a quick, sharp pinch like a syringe.

The couple that walked in looked like they were coming from the opera rather than a Broadway show. The young man wore a black tie, his platinum-blond hair was combed back, and the girl was in a light evening dress, her arms wrapped in long satin gloves. The dress revealed fading tan lines on the curve of her back.

"Forget Peter Luger, Andy, I want you to try the best thing in the world!" said the girl.

"Best thing in the world? You know I don't do speedballs anymore, honey." He stubbed out a cigar on the sole of his shoe. Then, noticing that she suddenly seemed uneasy, he reassured her. "I've never done a speedball, honey."

But that's not what had upset her. Seeing us, her eyes went cold. I'm sure that we must have seemed to her like a faded snapshot of a street in Rapallo: there was the miniature Indian, the huge, silent baker, and there I was too, my face covered in flour. That snapshot must have seemed so out of focus to her, so irreconcilable with her forty-two shining SL&B floors, with everything that she had achieved.

"I didn't know that you were in New York," Chloé whispered.

Something struck me in her tone of voice. I would have expected that she'd brag about her job, that she'd act as if the world was at her feet. Instead, she stood there, with her arms tight, a bit pained, as if she did care for us. In her eyes—when she raised them to look at me—was that sense of loss children have when their parents can't find their way.

"Among the thirty-three thousand restaurants in New York, did you really have to come here?" I asked.

"You're in Zagat," she said, smiling, trying to say something nice.

Sachin solemnly pushed a pan toward her. "This one is on the house."

"God, Chloé, you really do know everybody in New York!" said Andy. Laughing, he bit into the slice of focaccia before we'd had a chance to wrap it up. "From celebrities to pizza boys."

"Well," she said quietly, smiling at Sachin. "Thank you."

She took the bag and Andy the architect opened the door, which rang for one last time that night. And just like that, she was gone again.

Since the bakeries' balance sheets remained in the black, in May we decided to go to the other coast. It was a noncalculated risk. Martin, the bum-economist, from his grating on Sixty-first and Fifth, said that the equity/debt ratio was starting to tip and we were expanding too quickly. We paid him a good monthly retainer, but his latest reports were always the same one-liner: "You're not giving America time to poop: what goes in must come out!" Also the banks wanted more guarantees. Though we still had leases on our motorbikes, Queens Bank and Morgan Four Stones provided the financing to open seven new bakeries in California. Were we doing well or did the banks have to put money to work? It's funny, every time I walked inside a bank to get a loan, it reminded me of buying a pair of sandals in Rome: for the same pair there are three different prices (for tourists, for Italians, and for Romans); with their adjustable straps you can never tell if the sandals actually fit you; and if you don't have enough money, the owner says, "Just take them and pay me later, we know where you stay...and anyway we trust you." We pushed on faithfully.

The week before our L.A. opening Sachin— possibly believing we still lived in the seventies— plastered all of Sunset Boulevard with flyers saying "Forget LSD, Mom: Focaccia House!" We didn't really have a budget for Press & Advertisement. He was very proud of his idea.

The night before, when there was nothing left to be done, we decided to go to Malibu. We left our bags in a small B&B run by a guy from Marseilles, and before dinner, as we used to do in Rapallo, we jumped into the sea. It was seven o'clock on an evening in early May, and the days were becoming longer.

Marie Alice had on a one-piece bathing suit with a pattern of green circles, and she splashed at Sachin and Verger until they were running off along the shoreline. The water must have been really cold, as Don Otto too went into the ocean slowly, up to his thighs, jumping slightly when a wave came.

"First one who gets there gets a kiss!" shouted Marie Alice, pointing to an imaginary spot on the horizon.

Don Otto now was beating the waves. He was swimming calmly and listening to the nearby strokes, and when he turned his head to take a breath, she was next to him, her mouth half open in a yawn he would have liked to kiss. Damn, he liked swimming beside her.

And he didn't care if he made a fool of himself, and that he had never had a woman, and that she instead had been with who knows who or how many times.

"I won!" shouted Marie Alice, stopping arbitrarily mid-ocean, while Sachin and I were at least ten strokes behind her. Then she dove underwater like a silvery trout and emerged a few moments later. She handed to the baker her wet bathing suit clutched in her fist. "Here's your consolation prize."

A lock of red hair continued the smile on her cheek. Her legs lost their shape underwater.

"You didn't win. We arrived at the same time," said Don Otto, holding her bathing suit as if it were a real prize. "Or are you insecure?"

"C'mon, who wants to be with a retired porn star?" Marie Alice was laughing now. "And you, you're not giving me my first prize."

It would have been tough for anyone to make love in the ice-cold ocean that day, but not for Don Otto. He broke the waves.

Around eleven o'clock we ate on the terrace of the B&B facing the ocean. It was chilly, but it was a nice evening to eat outside. Some long, white clouds ran across the sky. The owner served an iced Chilean red wine and a lobster whose claws were still moving on the tray. At times a gust of wind blew out the candle in the middle of the table, and the owner would have to come and relight it.

Although it was eleven o'clock at night, the phone seemed to ring every minute. Inspired by Sachin's seventies-style flyers, a reporter had titled his piece in the *L.A. Times*: "Forget sex, drugs and rock & roll: Focaccia House!" and this had created a buzz. Sachin's idea had worked.

"No, I'm sorry, we're full," said the miniature Indian answering his cell phone and then hanging up.

"Why did you do that?" I asked.

"I know you're the CEO, Rosso...but what did we learn about street selling? To sell *fugassa* it's all about the *fugazi*," he said, playing with words: in Italian dialect *fugassa* means focaccia. He raised his finger and looked at us wisely. "To have a packed place you have to tell everyone the place is packed."

Sachin's cell rang again. I answered this time. "Who? One minute..." I covered the receiver and whispered, "It's Beyoncé herself, not even her PA... She's asking if she can come to our opening."

"Right, and I have Madonna on the other line," said Sachin, taking the phone away and turning it off. "It's just a prank."

The restaurant's landline rang. The owner brought over the receiver.

"Yes, I did hang up on you guys on purpose," said the miniature Indian answering. Then his complexion gradually changed color. After a few seconds he covered the receiver. "It...really...is...Beyoncé."

I noticed that his cheeks were bright red and the face of Lucien Verger, who was sitting next to him, was bright white. Together they looked like the Japanese flag.

"Franchising, home delivery, Beyoncé..." Don Otto shook his head as he lay the summer business plan down on the tablecloth. There was a shadow in his eyes. He had pronounced those words as if they weren't synonymous with victory, but with defeat.

"Don, you're not quitting, are you?" said Sachin, grimacing. "We're doing well."

"You're doing better than I ever did," said Verger, drying his egg-white nose.

"Yeah, thanks a lot...," said Sachin. "Don't you think we're doing well, Rosso?"

"We're doing okay." I smiled. And I felt that the five burgundy stripes on our family crest were shining again.

"You're doing something else, Rosso. You want to feed the entire world. But for me, Rapallo was enough," said Don Otto.

Perhaps because he had lost his virginity, the baker seemed articulate, certain, and aware. Marie Alice was sitting upright with her elbows pulled into her inexpensive evening dress, and now and then the wind rose, scattering a whirl of sand down the beach. Out there, the waves were breaking on the beach like uninterrupted applause.

· JOB 14 ·

Going Public

CHLOÉ VERDI

May 4, 2009, New York City

On June 3 a wire transfer to an offshore account listed as COA for"—the prosecutor turned and looked at the jury—"320 million dollars?" As he picked up the document, I shivered. "Are these transactions disclosed in the IPO prospectus, Ms. Verdi?"

CHLOÉ VERDI

July 7–August 31, 2008, New York City

W hen I dropped my raincoat on my desk around nine o'clock in the morning, there was an unusual degree of commotion in the office. The library was abuzz with obscure lingos such as Rule 10b-5, and green shoe, and I could hear people asking, "But is it true we're doing the offering?" The secretaries were letting their coffees get cold next to the phones, and I was told, "Buvlovski is waiting for you."

"Yes, it's an IPO on the New York Stock Exchange, Ms. Chloé Ombra Allegra Verdi," thundered Dimitri Buvlovski, slowly enunciating my name, as I walked into his office.

"An Initial Public Offering?" I asked without believing my own words. Was he asking me to work on an IPO, the listing of a company on the Stock Exchange, Buvlovski's number one obsession?

"One of the biggest deals of the year," said the Russian, taking a sip of coffee and then a sip of tea from the two cups in front of him. "Last week the company received a triple-A rating in the *Financial News*. Don't you read the *Financial News*, Ms. Verdi?"

I remained silent a moment, with my notepad open and the letters "AAA" rolling over my back like a marble. I still couldn't believe it.

"As a precedent for the prospectus I could use—" I said to show that I was prepared.

"Yes, please give any precedent to Mr. Zilberberg, who is in charge of drafting the prospectus. Instead, I would like for you to prepare a due-diligence checklist for this evening."

"What's the company name?"

"A food company," Buvlovski said, declining to give me the full picture in order to make my job more difficult, as was his practice.

As soon as I got back to my office, I quickly reviewed what an IPO was all about. First the bankers, who shop the company around, are selected. Then the due-diligence investigation begins to make sure that the company has no skeletons in its closet. As a result of the due-diligence search, the offering documents are prepared, including the prospectus describing the company and the securities being sold. Once a draft of the prospectus is in place, the company files the registration statement with the SEC for its review, comments, and approval. Then the road shows begin and the offering is pitched to potential buyers; pricing of the deal occurs; and finally the bell rings on the

New York Stock Exchange and the company is publicly traded.

Although the due-diligence was considered a bore, I threw myself into it without question. I was being given a task that was useful, actually important. I was working on the deal that the entire firm was talking about. Why me, the girl who was typically assigned to rearrange the library? I had no idea. I didn't even care that, just like Franz before him, Zilberberg was being assigned a job deemed more important than mine—and Zilberberg hadn't even passed the bar exam, while I had passed it last year.

Franz, Zilberberg, Andy—the architect I dumped Franz for—all the men I met within the firm or outside, were all cookie cutters. Their grand lifetime mission seemed to be the same: go to the Hamptons by sea plane, eat out at Nobu on Thursdays, and maybe in their fifties have their own assigned seat at Giants Stadium. Yes, even Andy, who initially had introduced himself as the next Frank Lloyd Wright, turned out to have fewer dreams than a palm tree.

Did I know any other kind of man, really? I thought of a face covered in flour in a small bakery off Broadway. I paused in my work and smiled. He was no longer a good-for-nothing.

Until now that world of Wall Street, which seemed so inaccessible from the outside, from the inside was a bit dull, made of mediocre people, with a predictable, mechanical life, primarily geared toward being part of the club. Maybe I had had too much time to think ... In fact, now that I was on the deal the entire firm spoke about, I thought that anybody would want to be me.

By the time Dimitri Buvlovski and I arrived at the St. Petersburg Café that evening, it was pouring. Generally, kickoff meetings took place at some Zagat-starred restaurant, though for IPOs Dimitri always books here—maybe it brought him good luck.

He enjoyed this place in the middle of nowhere on Coney Island, this eccentric Russian restaurant, in front of the ocean, which the police close down every six months. He liked the orange chandeliers, the aquarium in the shape of a grizzly bear with a couple of deep-blue fish swimming in it, and the disco mirror balls turning on the ceiling as in a seventies club. Above all, he liked that you could smoke at the table, which may also have been the reason the restaurant was closed down every six months. Because I was in charge of the due-diligence I had managed to convince Buvlovski to take me to the kickoff meeting with him.

"Your guest is arriving late because of the weather," said the waiter, refilling our glasses with Müller-Thurgau and opening a small square box of cigars.

"A Tuscan, please," said Buvlovski after a moment's thought.

"So, what do we know about the business?" I asked, trying to extract some information. "What is this, a phantom company?"

"Boston, Los Angeles, Chicago, ninety-seven stores, more than three new openings per day...it's such a fly-by-night company that in just a few months it's brought Domino's and Pizza Hut to their knees," said Buvlovski, breaking the silence.

"Oh, I think I saw something about it in the *Post*," I said, pretending to be in the know. The truth was that lately I had been working so hard doing useless stuff I barely knew anything about the outside world.

"And the *Financial News* and *People*. They're making more money than God! But we know nothing about them."

"So the newspapers know more about the company than we do?"

"I know, this is ridiculous," said Buvlovski. "It's the first time I'm listing a business on the Stock Exchange that's been around just seven months."

I let the wine wet my lips without drinking it. Since I don't generally drink, one glass on an empty stomach can put me in a daze, and in fact I was already quite dazed. I could feel my cheeks gradually becoming the same color as my Amaranth suit.

I grazed an imperfection on my glass's stem with my finger.

"Why did you involve me?" I dared to ask.

"The management is Italian. You're the only Italian-speaker in the firm."

"Imagine...an Italian friend of mine wanted to do the same thing, sell focaccia, and nobody would ever take him seriously."

"Well, you should have, Ms. Verdi," said Buvlovski. "You'd be sitting on the other side of the table now. You'd be the client."

I smiled. "No, I'd be on Sixth Avenue covered in flour."

Buvlovski smiled in return, because the wine seemed to be going to his head too.

"Why are you laughing, Ms. Verdi?"

I swallowed my laughter looking at the grizzly-bear aquarium. The clumsy Russian had annoyed me before; now he was almost fun. For a moment his intensity made him weirdly charming. I felt that strange attraction one sometimes feels for disgusting things, such as for the marrow of the osso buco. A rambunctious deep-blue fish kept banging against the glass.

"Why are you staring at the aquarium?" he asked.

"I may not look like it, but I'm the grizzly in the firm," I said.

"I thought I was the grizzly!" said Buvlovski, bursting into laughter.

Since he didn't want to order another bottle on an empty stomach, Buvlovski asked for the tea trolley. He also liked the St. Petersburg Café because of its infinite variety of teas. The white teapots lined up on the linen tablecloth looked identical to me, but the Russian confidently lifted a small samovar. "It's called the Prince Vladimir...," he said in a very low voice, pouring a cup for me and one for himself.

"It tastes of nutmeg," I said, sucking on my lower lip.

"Nutmeg, cumin, cloves, ginger..."

The more Dimitri listed the spices, the more handfuls of cumin, gusts of ginger, storms of Greek fennel seemed to fill the air, to cause our hands by mistake to brush against each other, and to narrow the space between our foreheads.

"Why do you keep on laughing, Ms. Chloé Ombra Allegra Verdi?"

At that moment, in the room the conversation halted and a couple of women who were seated at the entrance turned around to look. There was a hum of curiosity and gossip surrounding the young gentleman who had just entered the room.

"He's on the cover of *Vanity Fair*," one of the women said.

The young man held his wet raincoat on one arm, gracefully away from his body. I couldn't see his face from where I was seated, as he was handing something to the coat check guy. He didn't seem to have the butcherlike demeanor that businessmen typically have. He had an air of gentility, a slight awkwardness, that doesn't belong to the world of Wall Street. Then he headed toward our table.

Is it him? I wondered for a moment. I pinched a piece of skin on my arm. Did I have that much wine? It couldn't be him.

"I'm sorry about the rain," said Buvlovski, standing up and straightening out his jacket. "May I introduce Ms. Verdi, who is handling the due-diligence? This is the CEO of the company, Rosso Fiorentino..."

I felt a small shock travel through the bones of my neck and back and descend all the way down to my knees, which buckled as if they had been hit with a stick.

A few days later than scheduled, the due-diligence for the IPO of Focaccia House began at 1203 Sixth Avenue, the company's first Manhattan bakery. Although the company was opening three stores a day, all across the country, they did not bother renting an office, or more precisely, objected to it on a philosophical basis.

"This is not going to look good," the bankers had said. "It's going to look great. We're reinvesting profits back in the business, i.e., in new bakeries, not in useless office space." Management had responded on the advice of their consultant, a certain guy named Martin Marmeladov, someone nobody had ever seen or heard of and whose qualifications were unknown. That same guy was the one who had apparently advised the company to go public: "Time for an IPO," was the title of his handwritten memorandum on a paper napkin stained with stracchino cheese.

As instructed, the due-diligence was not carried out in an office, but in the bakery. While rhododendrons bloomed in the mild early summer air, we, the lawyers, were all crammed into a three-square-foot closet, next to an oven, sweating bullets, covered in flour, drowning in boxes. We were reviewing contracts and having a sauna at the same time.

Typically, in important deals, a data room is organized to gather the business's confidential information. The data room is not welcoming; this makes it difficult for the lawyers to discover the company's skeletons. Usually it has no windows, is flooded with boxes of useless information while the sensitive documents are hidden somewhere else, and the coffee tastes of pistachio. Well, here it was taken to an entirely new level. The typical data room was a five-star hotel suite compared with the inhumane closet we were drowning in.

"Do you need more water?" an employee named Alejandro Caselli would ask now and then, when we looked particularly dehydrated (as a result of our proximity to the oven, the room temperature was above 100 degrees Fahrenheit). His usual duty was to wrap up focaccia at the counter, but during the IPO he had been put in charge of the data room.

"We need to see these agreements," I said. Most documents I had been reviewing throughout the morning were useless, but I had discovered some interesting stuff in the board of directors' minutes. "Certain payments of $125,000 are made in cash, and $320 million has been wired to an offshore account listed as COA. What does COA stand for?"

"Miss, if you're not referring to the documents that the attorney, Mr. Zilberberg, is reviewing," said the employee hesitantly, "we would have to make a request with the management."

Joe Zilberberg, who was still waiting for his bar exam's results, was already an attorney in the employee's mind, while I, who had passed the bar a year earlier, was a "Miss."

"Wouldn't it be faster to speak with someone?" I asked.

The employee smiled. "The management is very busy. I doubt they're even around. Today's the road show, Miss..."

I quickly picked up the jacket of my suit (on which someone had rested a tray of sage focaccia) on my way to the road show.

"So, we are going back to the office?" asked Zilberberg, checking the time and noticing, relieved, that it was almost lunchtime.

Although he had been assigned the prestigious task of drafting the prospectus, commuting or having lunch was the most gratifying moment of Joe Zilberberg's day. Only when he was going from his home to the office, or in general any time when he was not working, for instance when he was hanging out at the firm's cafeteria, did his job seem to be important and prestigious. As soon as he started working, it made no sense. Since joining Buvlovski's group, he had already lost ten pounds and his girlfriend.

When I arrived at the road show at the Waldorf Astoria, the doormen were so busy directing traffic it could have been the opening of a nightclub in the meat packing district. The road show is the moment of truth in an offering, when you understand whether the market is buying, although nobody really ever knows what.

Under the Waldorf Astoria's flags, filling and emptying in the wind, journalists were lined up for security checks, while the heads of the funds were ushered in easily through a secret entrance.

"Last month shows a 62 percent gain in earnings per share over May," echoed the words in the Grand Ballroom.

After showing security my ID, I entered the room. On the podium Martin Case, Pyramid Capital's CEO, one of the IPO's lead underwriters, with his imperious blue eyes, was wrapping up his speech. For an instant his gaze met that of his high school friend in the audience—Mark Schwarz, the head of Fortitude Retirement Fund, whose feeder fund invested the savings of millions of Norwegian retirees.

"And the EPS gives us two different types of information," concluded Mr. Case. "First, in this country in June, people ate more focaccia than hamburgers. Second, health insurance stocks are skyrocketing." He flagged a paper to the Grand Ballroom. "Has anyone seen this report from Health & Science? A Mediterranean diet based on focaccia, two slices per day, lowers high levels of triglycerides..." He slowly opened and closed his hand as if he was waving to someone. "Goodbye strokes, first cause of mortality in the country! Ladies and gentlemen, this is a story the Street wants to hear."

In the second row, the journalists quickly jotted down the reference to Wall Street, while the rest of the audience already seemed satisfied and asleep. Even Harpers's CEO, nicknamed Red Eye because he had once brought the Stock Exchange to tears by barring a company's listing, was quietly chatting with his neighbor. The offering was already oversubscribed.

At the door my eyes wandered to the great crystal chandeliers above that underbrush of bankers and lawyers. The Grand Ballroom that each year hosted the debutantes' balls in white tie, now hosted the elite of finance. Instead of Chablis, waiters served Gatorade and coffee. Instead of chasing one another for a kiss, we exchanged business cards. Instead of dancing, people spoke about money. The hundreds of jackets and ties seemed freshly ironed below the mellow lights. Ever since that evening at the St. Petersburg Café, I had been feeling a vague sense of unreality, as if I had been run over by a car.

They were all seated in the first row. All of them but him. There was Sachin; the last time I'd seen him he was in a dingy bakery and before that on Rapallo's promenade with a sheet of sunglasses at his feet. There was Don Otto, the baker, and Franz was there too, as he always managed to work his way in everywhere. He had a badge pinned to his shirt that read CO-MANAGER NEW YORK OFFICE. Rosso's mother was standing near the side entrance, wearing a colorful hat unsuited to the occasion. She was leaning on the arm of a friend who had accompanied her from Italy and seemed stunned, as if she too had been run over by a car or a freight train.

"And what about him?" I asked the security guard standing behind me.

"Who?"

I pointed to the empty seat in the first row.

"Ah, the CEO...," smiled the guard dreamingly, absorbed in his well-groomed sideburns. "If I were him, I know where I'd be..."

Before the Q&A session started (the questions and answers with management), Rosso Fiorentino walked in and took his seat in the front row. Like a very important person who had no time to waste, he seemed to show up only when he was actually needed.

A t six o'clock in the evening on Monday, August 29, two nights before the IPO, everything seemed ready. In line with the Stock Exchange's recommendation, it had been decided to close the listing in August—and not in September—to discourage speculative behavior. Over the previous weeks, Buvlovski's desk had become a magnet attracting everything: reports of the New York Stock Exchange, comments from the SEC, a change of underwear for me, who hadn't been home since forever. By now, my three red Amaranth business suits were as dirty as a tablecloth at JG Melon's.

While Joe Zilberberg was reorganizing the due-diligence folders, I verified for one last time the risk factors on page twenty of the prospectus. I, instead of him, had been assigned to draft the prospectus because—to the surprise of the partners of the firm—I "knew" the management. I added as a risk factor: *"Management: Total Inexperience and Complete Lack of Business Judgment."*

Dimitri Buvlovski was stationed at his usual place, staring out of his office window. He rose to retrieve the sheet of paper that the fax had just spat out. A fax coming in from the SEC at this hour was not a good sign. If we didn't respond to it in time, the listing would slip.

"Management is not returning your calls?" he barked at the pigeons of Lexington Avenue. "It's typical that clients prefer to hang out with the bankers rather than responding to us. But I thought you knew those guys! Let's hope for you there's no biggy in this fax..."

The Russian took the prospectus from me and started quickly reading the questions from SEC. "It all seems inapplicable, good," he growled. "Section 5, litigation re intellectual property, inapplicable; accrued liabilities, inapplicable; Section..."

"I think that's applicable," I said, rubbing my eyes that wouldn't stay open anymore. "Certain payments are made in cash, and hundreds of millions of dollars are wired to an offshore account listed as COA. No idea what that stands for."

"The rest of the management isn't available either?" said Buvlovski, shaking his head.

"I don't know where they are."

"You better fix it. That's why I gave you the job...otherwise the listing slips."

When, later that evening, the jitney dropped me off in Bridgehampton, the city's mugginess had faded into fresh salty air. Every so often, a comforting smell of grilled corn came from a nearby barbecue. I had decided to go out of my way to save the IPO. Just as before I had tried to help Shimoto, now I was putting all at risk to save *his* dream. Even if it made me look ridiculous.

At Villa Fitzpatrick, where management was staying, the line of people waiting began in the parking lot. For that one evening, the residence of a Blackstone partner had been converted into a hotel. Everything had happened so fast; they didn't even have time to arrange for a proper reception center. The analysts were waiting in silence, while outside the bathroom two women journalists were exchanging gossip.

"Do you think Rosso goes to Bungalow 8 to pick up women?"

"He doesn't need to. He's going out with the world's biggest rock star."

"No, no, she's going out with his friend Franz. But did you notice whether she redid her tits?"

I took the villa's elevator to the fourth floor, management quarters. The reception hour was over, but when the security guard at the door saw my SL&B card, he let me in anyway. The hall was dark and the windows were open and rattling a bit from the wind outside. Either out of exhaustion or because of the semidarkness, for a moment I couldn't remember why I had come.

To go from "zero to hero" in the blink of an eye seemed to be the norm in these days. Very swiftly you could go from being a good-for-nothing to head of a Fortune 500, from being friends with bums and pornographers to friends with the stars. Success wasn't about school, experience, résumés, or curricula vitae; the only thing that mattered was who had the last laugh. And that last laugh—like getting a mortgage, having sex, learning how to day-trade, just like everything else—was made so easy for everybody, that everything was all much more difficult—including holding on to your own home and making sure that your boyfriend wasn't cheating on you with Silicon Valley's latest operating system.

In the dark hall, Sachin's small figure appeared wrapped in a Scottish robe.

"I see you prefer escorts to the Venus with the Singing Nipples," I said. Through a half-open door, I glimpsed two women half naked, wrapped in baby doll outfits, playing cards on a bed.

Sachin looked up as if the Chrysler Building was about to crash on his head.

"No," he said, laughing. "Nothing is crashing down yet. Except maybe on you, if you don't get this legal job done."

He was wearing a shark's-tooth necklace and holding a Budweiser.

"Two escorts?" I asked.

"Well, mine is the blond one . . . the other is Rosso's. I did stop searching for the Venus and I also stopped writing." Sachin took a sip of beer. The shark's teeth danced on his throat. "But it's just a break."

"Is he on the terrace?" I asked. "We need some important information, otherwise the stock listing slips."

"Rosso? He's out on the terrace. At your own risk."

I took a deep breath. "Is it true that he's going out with...a rock star?"

"After you crashed and burned him? He's done with girlfriends." Sachin smiled. "It's true, though, that she fancies him."

The terrace was dark, but the ocean beyond was flat and luminous, lit by the moon. In the strong breeze, tissue paper from a bouquet of flowers was floating across the tiles. I walked slowly, in my disheveled suit, reminding myself to take it easy and clutching at the prospectus under my arm.

"Is it Mardi Gras or an IPO?" laughed an angel's voice at the end of the terrace, commenting on my attire as I walked in. "Or is it the Carolina Herrera Fashion Show? Check out that ass! It defies the force of gravity..."

The world's biggest rock star was sitting right there, on a white chaise longue, next to the drink cart, her back against Franz's knees.

"Ciao," she said. To make up for her lukewarm welcome, she reached for the tray next to her and poured a glass of something, offering it to me with a friendly gesture. "Or perhaps you lawyers don't drink?"

"No, Chloé doesn't drink," Franz said in her ear.

In that moment a man in a gray Prince of Wales double-breasted suit stepped out from the half shadow.

"What are you doing here?" asked Rosso Fiorentino. His voice was brusque and controlled, as if he had just been operated on for appendicitis or was speaking to a low-level employee.

"But you didn't answer my question, Rosso," said the rock star, continuing to check me out as she got up from the chaise longue. "Are all your lawyers this hot?" She walked over to Rosso and adjusted his gray tie over his shirt. "You may be a prince of high finance, but you have no idea how to knot your own tie."

"You're in a jacket and tie," I said, squinting my eyes.

"He's always in a jacket and tie," said the rock star. "He has a videoconference in half an hour with Zurich."

"Why are you here, Chloé?" asked Rosso, lighting a table lamp on the terrace.

"I think . . .," I said, trailing off, lost.

At that moment, all at once, everything seemed senseless: the SX regulation, the reports of the NYSE, comments from the SEC, the steamy data room, and I myself and all of my pathetic efforts to save the IPO. And that Franz was going out with the world's biggest rock star, and that she was dating him, and not because they liked each other, but to be closer to that impossible speculative world of an enterprise richer than the GDP of a country—a world invented by a guy who couldn't even keep a dog on a leash, whom everybody ran after now, and who instead was hanging out with escorts.

I heard laughter on the terrace. "Your lawyers may be hot, but they're not that bright!"

This last slap in the face seemed to awaken me. "Yes, Rosso, I came here to ask you some questions."

When I was back in the office, it was five o'clock in the morning. No one was there, not even Buvlovski. The days were growing shorter and the sky was still pitch dark, except for some fading moonlight here and there. With whatever brainpower I had left, I reread the totally crazy answers I had received from Rosso during our two-minute conversation: "The payments in cash are made to a consultant named Martin. He is a bum and has no bank account, that's why we pay him in cash... The multimillion-dollar wires are to the Christ of the Abyss, that's what COA stands for... Why? I promised that I'd give him fifty cents for every dollar I made."

I tried to transcribe them in somehow legal terms. "The payments listed hereunder are to a consultant who has requested to be paid in cash. The wire transfers to the COA bank account are to a not-for-profit entity, pursuant to a grant the Company wishes to honor."

I faxed everything back to the SEC.

On August 31 Rosso Fiorentino rang the opening bell of the New York Stock Exchange and Focaccia House became publicly listed. People, and the Street, believed in a business that created more jobs than tech companies, and even more jobs than McDonald's. The banks were happy to invest in a product that you could smell, touch, and eat, as opposed to impalpable software. Insurance companies saw their profits skyrocket with a diet not based on red meat and that decreased the risk of heart attacks. And frankly who wouldn't invest in the business after trying a slice of Don Otto's?

Focaccia House's IPO surpassed the one for VISA, which had taken place just a few months earlier. It was the largest IPO in U.S. history.

Rosso Fiorentino, the Businessman

CHLOÉ VERDI

May 4, 2009, New York

D id you love Rosso Fiorentino, or did you want to take his place?" asked the prosecutor. I suddenly realized his terrifying strategy.

"In those days everybody wanted to be Rosso Fiorentino," I said. "Even Rosso himself."

ROSSO FIORENTINO

Labor Day 2008, New York City

W hen I walked out on the terrace this morning I had a good feeling, just as I had on the day I started Focaccia House. I was in my pajamas and the sun was rising over Central Park. I could hear the distant whistle of the skyscrapers waking up, wind scraping against steal, *sling, sling,* that sound slot machines make when the coins are coming down. The gray and pink air over Harlem suggested the beginning of a hot summer day. For the briefest moment I thought I could do some writing, but the thought quickly vanished. While Franco was opening the terrace's blue awning, Elena rested a tray with coffee and the papers on the table.

I had flown Elena and Franco over from Italy; they had worked for my parents some years ago and were looking for jobs. Franco specialized in cooking Southern Italian cuisine and Elena (who had also been my nanny) Northern Italian cuisine; her hand-made agnolotti were unbeatable. I now no longer heard old Greeks snoring, or the rattle of the N train in the distance. I occupied a $160 million penthouse at 240 Central Park South, but according to the IRS, I was living beneath my means. "At least get yourself a fucking penthouse, if you want to look like a respectable CEO," had been Martin's recommendation.

I had hired an up-and-coming interior designer named Alexandra Sharpe, asking her to furnish the place to make me look like a CEO. I was terrified, though, that she might actually be able to do that. I guess that was my problem: Did I want to look like someone I didn't want to be? Do something great and beautiful, the Maestro had said. Had I succeeded? Was this it?

And if so, why did I continue to hear demons inside? A coma is like exposing film to the sun before the image can be printed: I couldn't remember anything about those ten minutes that, seven years ago, had defined my life and taken that of Marinella, the woman I loved. According to the police report I was driving on the wrong side of the road. Why was I passing a car while a truck was coming at full speed in the other direction? The combined impact of the two vehicles in the collision was 120 miles an hour. Why was I driving into a wall at 120 miles an hour? According to the police report my alcohol level was zero. Why was I soberly going full speed into death? The money I was now making was not answering any of these questions.

After the car accident I decided to change. I stopped going to parties. I was no longer a good-for-nothing and had rolled up my sleeves. The company I had founded was a success. So why were the demons still here, maybe louder than ever? Had I not changed?

Alexandra Sharpe, the very talented interior designer I'd hired, had first furnished the penthouse with microfibers, blue couches, and dragonfly Tiffany lamps. "There," she said. "You now look like a high-powered CEO...not cool?" Seeing my hesitation she had tried Sven grass-green sofas and Meurice rectangular chandeliers. "Or are you looking for the sophisticated executive type?" Because I wasn't convinced, she transitioned to Venetian Gothic with yellow damask pillows and Murano lamps. "See, the beauty and imperfection of the Venetian Granita marble kind of gets it, no?" Still sensing some hesitation on my part, she refurnished the entire house in an Ottoman Turkish style. "Look," she said at some point. "I know you've paid my full commission, but we're getting nowhere. Do you want me around so that you can peek up my skirt?" she asked peacefully, without resentment. "And if it's not even that, I have no idea what we're doing here. I don't have the faintest clue what type of CEO you want to be." She ended up conceding that the best decision was to leave the place completely empty, and I should go out and buy myself some art.

"And this," said Elena, withholding a smile, placing a letter on the tray next to the papers, in the bright Manhattan dawn.

I signed the H1-B immigration visa petition letter, and took a sip of coffee.

"Wonderful. Now my nephew will be working for Don Otto as well!" Elena said, clapping her hands.

"I don't know if it's wonderful," I said. "Anyway, he'll be working for Adam. Don's left."

"Well, he's in love," said Elena, tidying her gray hair that was turning white. "I too would rather be in love than make money. And you, Rosso, when are you going to find yourself a nice girl instead of going out with prostitutes? There are a lot of nice girls in New York."

"But they're more expensive than the prostitutes," I objected reasonably.

"You've changed. You think only about money."

It was six o'clock on a Monday morning when I arrived at the office. Sixth Avenue was oddly empty, and the streetlights were uselessly turning green. Once my life had been about going from one party to the next; now it was all about work. I walked inside our offices at 1203 Sixth Avenue, which were sitting on top of our first Manhattan bakery. I straightened my ash-gray double-breasted jacket in front of the mirror's elevator. Had I really changed? After cleaning up my desk, I checked the futures on Focaccia

House's ticker (FH) in the *Wall Street Journal*, + 0.47. Yes, I have changed, I thought, relieved by how meticulously I was reviewing the data. The phone rang.

"Delivery for you," said the tired, rough voice of our security guard.

"What is it? I'm not expecting anything," I said.

"Breakfast. Focaccia."

Even though I had already had breakfast, I couldn't say no. I hated wasting food, especially focaccia. I walked into the empty hall. I watched the light of the elevator tick off each floor one by one with a ring. As the elevator doors slid open, the delivery boy walked out and said, "Promotional offer!"

I looked in my pockets for two dollars plus tip. "Here you go."

The delivery boy energetically shook his head, which was hidden under a visor, refusing the money, and pulled the package from his satchel. The package brushed against the white T-shirt with Focaccia House emblazoned on it. The T-shirt slightly bounced. It was actually a delivery girl. The uniform was a bit tight and I could make out two firm breasts unsupported by a bra just below the white cotton.

"Promotional offer!" she repeated, refusing even to take the tip.

"Look, Miss," I said, beginning to lose my patience. "I didn't order any breakfast and there is no promotional offer."

Then from under the visor she looked at me, and I recognized the petroleum-green eyes that had carried away our generation. Now they sparkled, clearly but a bit tired, like the sea in September.

"How did you know I was here?" I asked.

"Where else would you be?" said Chloé. "Do you like my new uniform? I fired myself."

"You fired yourself?"

"Kidding. I'm just on a leave, I got a bit burned out by your IPO... but you're not telling me if you like my new uniform."

"I like it," I said, smiling. I looked at the white T-shirt with Focaccia House emblazoned across the front. "Maybe it's a little tight."

She lowered her eyes, fixing them on the laces of her gym shoes. "Do you want to have breakfast with me in Central Park?"

"I have a lot of work to do."

"Come on, Rosso, it's Labor Day."

So we walked out toward Seventh Avenue, where there was now the usual late-summer activity. People were starting to arrive from the suburbs, and the police were blocking off Fifth Avenue to let the parade pass by. It was a hot, windy morning. I don't know why I felt out of place being there with her and not being behind my desk working—just as in the past I would have felt uneasy without a gin and tonic in my hand. We didn't talk much. Now and then, she tossed her visor up into the air and caught it coming down. Then she pointed to the steps of the University Club, where two barefooted men were eating a tray of sage focaccia.

"See, that there is a promotional offer...you're giving out free food!" said Chloé with a little cry; with her enthusiasm she manipulated the world, but no longer me. "It's all over the papers that Focaccia House's stands are feeding the bums across the five boroughs."

She picked up the visor off the ground, which, this time, she had missed coming down.

"It's all free publicity," I said.

"Feeding three thousand bums a day?" she said, unconvinced. "A first-rate ad agency like BBDO would cost you a third of the price."

"BBDO would cost the same and is not entirely tax deductible. Didn't you go to the University of Chicago?"

Chloé covered her eyes from the sunlight to look at me. "You've changed, Rosso."

We continued down Seventh Avenue toward Broadway. The sun was already strong and it shimmered over the hot dog vendors' stands. It was one of those days when you wish to be in love, but I could only hear the harsh sound of my own voice. I had spoken to her as if she were my employee. Now and then we walked into a shop, then out again onto the dirty sidewalks of Broadway beneath the billings for the musicals. She stopped in front of a red Spider Man's cape that was blowing in the wind on the corner of Forty-second Street and Seventh. The shop was a mix between a costume store and a video rental.

"I've never seen it," said Chloé. A broken light barely lit the inside. "I've never seen your film."

"What film?"

"I've done my due-diligence, remember?" she said with a defiant look.

"There's nothing to see."

"There's a lot to see!" She laughed. "It's a porn movie. Do you think it's out on DVD?"

Even though I had learned to be afraid of desires, she looked at me in the same way she had looked at me that night on the promenade in Rapallo, against the railing, the moment before she kissed me. This time, I felt nothing. Also her breasts bouncing under her T-shirt left me unmoved. I *have* changed, I thought, comforted.

"It's better if you see if SL&B will take you back."

"Rosso, how could you be a star in a porn film?"

"I was an extra," I said, and started walking again.

By the time we strolled down the last stretch of Broadway, it was almost evening. Chloé had spent the day going inside every shop on Sixth Avenue, trying on flip-flops, baseball caps, and all of the Uniqlo's sweaters on sale, but without buying anything.

I was still trying to find a way to get rid of her, or to have her disappear. The skyscrapers on Central Park South were lighting up in a checkerboard pattern. Dark gray clouds were regrouping in the sky for a last summer storm.

"And now, where are you going?" she asked. "It's dinnertime and we still haven't had breakfast. And it's about to pour."

When I stepped down below the grating in front of the Pierre Hotel on Sixty-first and Fifth, the usual smell of pot was floating up. The joint now looked like a cross between a storage space and a home office, with its flat-screen TV, the new iBook computer, and a laser printer. I immediately noticed, however, that the moving company had not followed my instructions. The Crate & Barrel's boxes were piled up next to the iron ladder while the one with the pricey Claremont double-deck glass coffee table had been opened.

"Why did they leave everything here?" I asked.

"I told them to do so," said Martin, the bum-economist.

He was sitting on the pricey crystal table and was gazing at the fishnet—which in theory was supposed to decorate the top of the coffee table, and which instead he had hung just below the grating, so that it would catch the cigarette butts and chewing gum that passersby threw down.

"It looks like an art display in a loft. Don't you think?" said Martin, pointing to the fishnet catchall.

"Why did you tell them to leave everything here? They were supposed to take everything away..."

Martin crossed his legs on the glass coffee table. "How much did you spend on all this stuff, four hundred grand?"

"You told me that if I wanted to look like a successful CEO, I needed to get myself a penthouse. Do you think that a credible financial consultant lives under a grating?"

"I have no incentives to leave. I have the chicest grating in town."

Just as I was slowly transitioning into being a CEO, he was taking his time transitioning out of being a bum.

"Let's see," I said as I took out my cell phone, "if the NYPD has a better incentive plan and kicks you out."

"I'm kidding," he said. "Tomorrow the moving company is carting everything to the place you got me in Astoria." He looked out onto the sidewalk at Chloé with her black, loose hair, who was tossing her visor up under the first drops of rain and who was still waiting for me. Then he picked up two pieces of paper that resembled our company's balance sheet. He must have printed them off the Internet from our Edgar filing with the SEC. "Keep your eyes on the numbers,

Rosso. You're expanding too quickly. You're taking on too much debt."

We arrived at 240 Central Park South completely soaked. My double-breasted jacket had turned into an exotic salad—dressed with Norway maple leaves and mud—and her T-shirt clung to her skin and was see-through. Chloé had refused to disappear and now wanted a tour of my house. When the elevator doors opened onto my apartment, our ears popped from the change in pressure. As a good-for-nothing, you may take a certain pride in showing your nine-bedroom apartment. I diligently walked her through the completely empty penthouse, across the Tuscan tile floors (the sole contribution of my interior designer), in front of the old masters' paintings (which I had purchased from a Manhattan gallery—can you imagine that they cost less than a Damien Hirst?), in front of the El Greco, the Cranach the Elder, the Rosso Fiorentino (to whom I owed my stage name), and through the oleanders, which I had planted inside the library to impress the escorts. When the tour was over, though, so too was the fun.

I could do some writing at The Deck, or go and see McEnroe, I thought randomly as she disappeared inside a powder room to change. I remembered I had tickets for the Senior Tournament at Madison Square Garden that night. Could I go and leave her here? You can lose all the money, but never lose your manners, my father always said. To my surprise, while Chloé freshened up, I began to groom myself with great care. I slipped inside a light end-of-summer gabardine suit, put on a pigeon-blood-red Battistoni tie, and squirted Drakkar Noir (which I no longer inhaled but used conventionally as cologne) on my wrists—perhaps too much care for an over-fifty tennis exhibition. But if I invite her, she'll think that I'm still into her. I went to sit on the terrace.

The opening of the terrace's glass door interrupted my thoughts. If she had walked into the powder room as a delivery boy, she emerged as a cross between a Whiskey Park waitress and a Ghirlandaio Madonna. She was naked up to her thighs, wearing only a white monogrammed shirt of mine that she must have found somewhere. On her head she had tied a towel. A few curls fell out, along the white line of her neck, like a handful of problems.

"Wow, we're up high," said Chloé with a little cry, letting herself fall on one of the terrace's deck chairs. "The house is a bit empty though. Maybe an interior designer could come in handy..." She paused in our awkward silence. "You could at least offer me a ginger ale. I did save your IPO, after all."

I took out the bottle of Drakkar Noir from my jacket's pocket.

"Okay, no ginger ale," she said. "Why are you not saying anything?"

I read the instructions on the back of the Drakkar Noir bottle, searching for the words.

"You didn't like me when I was broke," I said. "You like me now that I'm rich."

"I liked you when you were broke. I didn't like that you were spoiled."

"What's the difference?" I asked.

"Maybe I should go," Chloé said, standing up. "There's a party downtown at nine."

Although I had been hoping all day that she would leave, at that moment I felt a stitch somewhere between my chest and my lungs.

"Where are you going, to see Franz, Andy, or Buvlovski?" Suddenly all the words were coming out at once.

"It was better when you didn't say anything."

"Or are drugs enough for you?"

The wind had pushed away the black clouds, and five stars appeared at the far end of Central Park above the Reservoir. They formed an *O* with a crooked accent.

"Drugs?" said Chloé. She rolled the sleeves of my shirt up to her elbows and pointed one by one at the scars, which remained visible on her arms. "You mean antibiotics."

Now the rage seemed to have flown from my face into hers, and a tear cut her cheek. "You thought I was an addict? You thought I shot up? Yes, I shot up with antibiotics. You want to know why?"

In the air freshened by the storm the moment of truth had come. I looked deep into her eyes, which I couldn't understand, for which I had gotten rich and sold myself, those eyes I had pursued to the ends of earth, and which were still fleeing to some downtown party.

"My mother called off my thirteenth birthday party because I had a headache. In October I was pulled out of my first year of high school. It was not just headache. My neck and knees were swollen like watermelons and when I woke up one morning, my headache was so strong that my jaws were moving by themselves. So we started with the doctor game. We saw doctors and doctors, but they couldn't understand. We tried treatment after treatment, but they didn't work. Each time we saw a new doctor, he would prescribe another course of antibiotics, another dose of drugs."

Chloé lowered her forehead as though it was all her fault. "By the end the nurse couldn't find a good vein on my arm."

Near the five stars above the park, another star appeared. Now they formed a lion. And at each word she spoke, the lion seemed to take a step into the middle of the sky.

She spoke quickly. "I remember the sound of the mattress every time the nurse turned my body to the side so that I wouldn't get cheloids on my heels. It seemed that my mattress was made of cobs. If you only knew what it is like to be in bed at thirteen, fourteen, fifteen, sixteen . . . to see your mother sitting there, and your friends speaking quietly in your room because they don't want you to know what you're missing, who they're seeing tonight, where they're going on holiday. I was always in the same bed I was the day before, the month before, the year before. By the time they finally isolated the bacterium, my parents' insurance had long since run out. I had a variant of Lyme, which, back then, was not known at all."

"Lyme disease?" I asked. I didn't know much about it either. "So, that's why you finished high school in one year and university in two?"

"Yes, when I was back on my feet. And that's why I was in India as a journalist to try to make some extra money, and the Mickey Mouse crimes like dognapping to pay for the law school. After six years of private clinics, my parents were broke. I'm still sending money home now. And that's why I never went to parties, and I can't dance, and I don't drink." She was choking back her tears. "And why—"

"But how long were you in bed?" I asked.

Now her beautiful green eyes, rimmed by a bit of makeup, were neither happy nor sad. They looked like two fish underwater at Pozzetto beach.

"From thirteen to nineteen."

I caressed the scars in the hollow of her arm, her best years forever taken, and pulled down her shirtsleeves.

At that moment I understood why I had chased her to the ends of the earth. After I kicked off my shoes on the terrace, I ejected my light gabardine suit and tied my tie to a deck chair.

"Why are you stripping?"

"I want to be even," I said, wearing only my monogrammed shirt. I threw my boxers—crunched in a ball—as far as I could, and climbed onto the railing.

"What are you doing? Are you crazy?"

Chloé ran to the railing and grabbed my arm.

Ten, nine, eight, I started counting, just like when I dove down from very high up to reach the Christ of the Abyss. Fuck, I'm up high now, I thought, looking at Essex House, the proud flags of the Plaza Hotel, the dark and luminous teeth of the great city of desires that had welcomed me. Five, four... I was still in time. Three, two... Not to go for her. But I dove. On her bruises, in her petroleum-green eyes, between her lips.

The Frying Pan/
The Wedding

CHLOÉ VERDI

May 4, 2009, New York City

I s this a love story, Ms. Verdi, or a Ponzi scheme?"
asked the prosecutor.

ROSSO FIORENTINO

September–October 2008, New York City

Primrose's funeral took place on a clear September morning, at Don Otto's, who now lived on a forty-acre estate near East Hampton. We were all in the garden, dressed in black suits, accessorized with long, burgundy-colored neckties, and only Marie Alice was missing. The baker slowly emptied out the pot and put the flower to rest in the shade of a large oak. Now the petals, no longer strong and purple, had a soft pink color. They were almost transparent.

"Here you go, Primrose…," said Don Otto, tossing another handful of earth on top of the stem, and a big, fat tear danced in the corner of his eye.

On the very same evening the baker had knelt on the white sand at Sag Harbor and proposed to Marie Alice, the gardener had said, "This flower's sick," as though it knew that Don Otto's heart had room for just one.

As a sign of mourning, after Primrose's funeral, the wedding preparations were put on hold for a few days. Then they resumed more frantically than ever before, growing more complicated than a restructuring of Focaccia House.

At first the bride and groom thought of holding the reception at La Cervara in Italy, where some elegant weddings took place in the nearby fourteenth-century abbey, but it was too complicated. Then they discussed getting married at Marie Alice's house in Queens, but the garden was too small for dancing. So they started visiting some hotels downtown and found a free Saturday at the Puck Building on 295 Lafayette Street.

"I don't know," said Marie Alice, leafing through the thirty-two-page HP inkjet glossy brochure. "I don't want to be married someplace where thirty couples get married every year."

So they stopped talking about where and started discussing the rest, hoping that by discussing the rest they would resolve where: Shall we do a buffet or a seated dinner? Assigned seating, or just a sit-down without assigned seats? And how are the ushers greeting the bridal party outside the church? No, they're not throwing rice, it chokes the pigeons! Right, and what should the ushers wear? Can you believe that all the churches in Manhattan are booked through October?

One Friday evening in early September, when they were about to give up forever on the idea of getting married, they found themselves sharing nachos at the Frying Pan, at Pier 66 Maritime in Chelsea. The glorious ship that had once served during the American Civil War was now demoted to a nightclub. The plastic tables had been beautified with pots of violets that looked just like Primrose's city cousins.

"Should we have candlelight?" asked Don Otto looking down anxiously, as he did when he was kneading and there were thirty pans to bake before dawn.

"Candlelight is a major enterprise!" snorted Marie Alice. Then she drew the baker to her and kissed him on the mouth. "Okay, okay, we can have candles."

The Frying Pan was the chosen venue.

When the bride and groom left the St. Demetrios Cathedral in Astoria, Queens, it was a warm, clear October day. Handel's Ave Maria poured softly out of the central nave into the street, and outside the ushers blew soap bubbles instead of throwing rice. Sachin and Federico followed Marie Alice, each holding a corner of the longest veil. Federico, the now sixteen-year-old painter, had come all the way from Italy for the occasion; with his curly blond hair he looked just like an angel flown down from the golden altar. Then the newlyweds jumped into the limousine and we all drove to the Frying Pan to the honking of horns.

Because they hadn't agreed on the dress code, the invitation said *chic, but not in jeans*, but nobody knew what that meant, which created some level of chaos. It looked like a costume party rather than a wedding. The guests wore everything from tuxedoes to cutaway morning jackets as if it were a British wedding, to white ties and tails as if it were an Austrian wedding, to a Battle of Berezina Russian military uniform (Buvlovski), and there was one orange-popsicle-colored attire and matching top hat (Sachin, given the importance of the color orange in Hinduism). Other guests—the more elegant ones, like Franz—showed up in white linen suits.

Given that there was no seating chart, at around six o'clock everyone sat at a table of their own choice. Don Otto and Marie Alice had reached an honest, yet not entirely practical, compromise: a nonassigned sit-down dinner with a small buffet for the cheeses. Some seating worked well (Franz next to David Jeffrey, given their randomly discovered common passion for imperialism and shared view that the United States should take over Canada); some seating worked better (Chloé's old Chicago roomy Juncal to the left of Buvlovski) than others (Lucien Verger to the right of Buvlovski). Cesar the publisher and Miranda and Anna Carlevaro, whom Sachin had insisted on inviting from Italy, were a bit pissed because they all ended up at the same table, and therefore weren't able to meet anyone. Miranda was talking about quitting the publishing world and starting a business competing with Focaccia House (she discussed the pros and cons of farinata, a type of Italian pancake made with chickpea flour).

"I always wondered about Tajikistan's economy," said Buvlovski at some point during the main course, sitting stiffly in his great-grandfather's Battle of Berezina Russian military uniform. "Who are your clients?"

"Farmers," said Juncal, who was displaying the most vibrant tan of the party.

"Farmers? So what can your hourly rate possibly be?"

"Goat milk yogurt, solyanka, and lemon cake." Juncal nodded. "But on weekends we also get to smoke free pot in the mountains."

Lucien Verger raised his index in question mode. "May I squeeze in an idea?"

"Please pay no attention, Mr. Buvlovksi," said Marie Alice, elbowing Verger, who had seated himself next to her. "For sixteen years he's been saying he wants to change his job."

"Well, it's been six months that I've wanted to change my job too!" said Buvlovski laughing.

"Trust me, Dimitri, my new idea is a clean business," repeated Lucien Verger, drying his long white nose. "Porn has disappointed me."

They all wanted to change jobs, except for Cesar, who promised he would die as a publisher.

As the sun was setting and the skyscrapers' reflection in the ocean faded, I continued watching for Chloé. She said she might be arriving late, I reassured myself. After Chloé had finished her leave and returned to SL&B, they'd been working her hard. We had been dating a couple of nights, but the mornings after she turned down my invitations to have coffee together at Via Quadrono. Were we going out? Or was it just sex? In New York it seemed easier to sleep with a girl than to have breakfast with her.

At the end of dinner, silence descended over the Frying Pan. A jukebox, which had been placed on the boat's stern, began to play "The Blue Danube." Don Otto, with his round eyes sharpened, stood before Marie Alice, who had orange blossoms in her red hair and a tremulous smile. After looking at each other for a moment as though they were meeting for the first time, they started dancing a waltz; slowly and a bit stiffly at first, trying to remember the steps, then more quickly. Now they were going fast, feeling more carefree and confident, and the waltz increasingly resembled a tango. No one had ever seen Don Otto so wild, especially when he picked up Marie Alice and held her in the air, and she so demure and happy.

I walked somewhere quiet, near the bow of the boat, to take a work-related call (the banks urgently wanted to discuss refinancing). The water was gently breaking against the hull. The wood on the deck squeaked. I was not alone. A white linen suit, which looked just perfect under the moonlight, had followed me. Why was Franz here? He was holding a cool glass of champagne. He waited patiently while I finished my call.

"Good to see you," I said after hanging up.

"Well, the truth is that I crashed the wedding," Franz said, reaching out and resting the cold champagne glass on my cheek for a moment.

"I'm sure you were on the list," I said, embarrassed. "You're the master of parties. You're always invited. Do you still party?"

"Of course." Franz smiled. "Working for you guys is just a hobby. And you, did you finish your novel? Remember I gave you a pen in the hospital, on your nineteenth birthday, after the crash?"

The master of parties opened his silver cigarette case and lit himself a Belomorkanal, one of those Russian cigarettes we used to smoke together at times. Exhaling a familiar-smelling plume, he looked sideways at me.

"Well, we could write a book about this story together," Franz added. "At least no one has died this time. We're merely crushing the world's economy."

I couldn't understand. Was he saying that we were not doing a good job, or was he just envious? Or did he want me to feel guilty?

Suddenly, through his cigarette's alabaster-colored smoke I could see the amber hair of Marinella, whom we both had loved, whom I had taken from Franz, and then from the world, with a wrong turn.

"Will you do the same with Chloé?" he asked, as if he could read my mind. I noticed his pained smile; he had lost his invincibility. Maybe he was still hurting because HWBC had fired him, or because Chloé had dumped him, or maybe because he was now working for me, and we had traded places, and for the first time he was losing and I was winning. He stared at me with dark sad eyes and, by doing so, turned the knife in the wound that all the worldly success possible could never heal.

"You think I did it on purpose?" I asked. "You think I killed Marinella on purpose?"

"You don't do things on purpose, Rosso," he said. "In your world all things happen by accident, like the empire you built."

Franz offered me a Belomorkanal.

"No thanks," I said.

"Look, it's not enough to quit smoking," Franz said, lighting a cigarette for me anyway. "It's not enough to make money."

round nine o'clock the cake was served: a forty-seven-layer whipped cream cake in the form of the skyscraper on Sixth Avenue in which Focaccia House had its headquarters.

How could she be so late?

"And what is that girl's name over there?" asked Marie Alice. "She looks like a princess."

"I don't know," said Don Otto. "She must be a friend of Federico's."

"You've invited so many people, you don't even know who's here!" The bride laughed.

"Virginia. I didn't invite her," said Federico, startling.

And there she was, at the entrance of the deck wearing a necklace of semiprecious stones, as if she had somehow been invoked by our discussion of Marinella. Every time I saw her, I was reminded of how much she and her sister Marinella looked alike; her neck's white line, her grace, her hair, which spread about her shoulders like snakes of gold. She could have been seventeen or eighteen years old by now and she wore a white organza dress.

"I'm in New York with family, visiting. We saw the wedding announcement; it was all over the papers." She smiled. "But I didn't know if you would be here."

"Here, from the bride," said Federico, holding out a plate of cake.

The sixteen-year-old painter had made a beeline across the deck when he recognized Virginia. Federico was so nervous he kept adjusting his hearing aid, which kept on whistling, as ever.

Virginia accepted the plate out of politeness. "Thank you, but my cousin is waiting downstairs. We have tickets for *Mary Poppins*."

"Do you still go to Portofino?" asked Federico, holding his breath.

"And do you still paint?" Virginia smiled, looking at him. "You know I still have your painting in my bedroom."

She may as well have written the word "painting" on the sixteen-year-old painter's stomach. Summoning the courage, Federico rested his hands on her smooth hips.

"And did you save your dad?"

"Not yet!" said Virginia, laughing. "But he likes your painting too." The young girl put down the plate with the cake, so that she could slip her arms around Federico's neck. "Maybe we can save him together."

Seeing that there was nowhere else to go, the painter kissed her.

When I went back to the deck everybody was dancing. Verger was dancing with Miranda, asking her how you become a publisher, Juncal was teaching Buvlovski to stay loose on his feet, Sachin was talking to Cesar about his writer's block, and Franz was waltzing to a song by the Throwing Muses. All tanned, in a white linen suit, he was once again the master of this spectacle. Don Otto and Marie Alice were dancing like two people in love.

"Don't they look like Premi and Kamu?" a voice whispered in my ear. I jumped. I remembered a night graced by the Maestro many weddings ago. I turned around.

Chloé wore a simple green cotton dress with a splash of yellow that matched her eyes, which were beautiful and a bit cold. She held a big file under her arm.

"Sorry, I was stuck in the office," she said.

"Until now?"

"Actually, I've been here for a while, looking for you."

"Do you want to dance?" I hesitated. I took the big folder from her hands and put it somewhere safe.

I felt the hesitation of when two lovers who have been chasing one another finally get together, and the obstacles have been overcome, the oceans crossed, the mountains climbed, and the only obstacle left is whether the two lovers will be capable of loving each other. In Italy she didn't want to dance. Here in New York I discovered why. Will she dance with me now?

"Dancing. I hope you won't go dancing in Rome! I heard you guys are opening in Italy," said Lucien Verger with his usual bad timing, handing me a glass of champagne. "To the newlyweds!" He poured some of his champagne into Chloé's half-full glass and then raised his in a toast. "Aren't you guys expanding too much?"

"To the newlyweds!" said Chloé, wetting her lips. Then she turned to me. "You've decided to go to Rome? Are you McDonald's now? C'mon, don't be silly, let's go dance instead... Will you teach me?"

And the way she turned to me and smiled, I understood that it was not just sex. Not for either of us.

Around three in the morning, the bride and groom took off in a white-and-orange limousine, and the couples started to go home. Chloé too left because the following day she had to be in the office early. It had been a beautiful wedding. The waiters were making fewer and fewer rounds with hot chocolate and rum, and suddenly dawn came. I was no longer used to partying so late. Federico and I were the last ones there and kept on walking in circles, arm in arm, passing between us a bottle of retsina we had found in the kitchen.

We were both drunk, happy, and discombobulated each in our own way: Federico by that one first kiss you never forget, and I by a second chance at love that I never thought I'd get.

· JOB 17 ·

The Meltdown

CHLOÉ VERDI

May 4, 2009, New York City

On July 3, 2008, 620 million dollars was wired to an offshore account labeled COA; on August 7, 840 million dollars was wired to the same COA account; on September 9, 1.2 billion dollars..." The prosecutor approached my witness stand. "Aren't COA your initials, Ms. Chloé...Ombra...Allegra?"

ROSSO FIORENTINO

November–December 2008, Rome

We were seated on the top floor at 5 Via Condotti, a Late Renaissance Italian palazzo in Rome facing the Spanish Steps that now hosted five wood-fired ovens. I had succumbed to the temptation of the McDonald's strategy: to continue to grow the company and buy bakeries even if things were slowing down; to continue to "eat up" potential competitors in order not to be eaten up and to keep the banks on my side.

"Annibale Carracci, sixteenth-century master, commissioned by Cardinal Odoardo Farnese." I pointed to the fresco on the ceiling, trying to use what my father had taught me of Italian art to distract the board of directors from the balance sheet's footnotes. The directors looked up and the red angels in the fresco—the cherubim—looked back down at them.

"Carracci," said an unconvinced Gunter Vint, also known as Gunny, the representative of the Swiss Banks. His ash-blond hair was perfectly combed and parted on the left, and he kept on pressing it with his hand. We later discovered that he suffered from a (severe) hypersensitive scalp disorder. "But what is a Carracci doing in a bakery?"

"The same can be asked of you, Gunter," I noted.

"Easy answer," he replied with his chirpy Swiss accent. "I'm here to advise the banks whether they should extend additional credit to your company or not."

"Yes, I think he is," Federico whispered in my ear, adding to our suspicion that Gunter gave off bad energy.

I pressed the Drakkar Noir bottle against my lip. Because it didn't have the desired effect of relaxing me, I looked outside the window and tried to breathe in all the remaining glory from the 135 Spanish Steps. But once my eyes readjusted to the indoor lights, my confidence was gone again. At the end of the boardroom the irresistible Monday morning smile of seven U.S. bankers was appearing on a screen. They were all sitting in a large videoconference room in New York.

"Midterm debt is skyrocketing and sales are dropping," said a voice from the screen. "Why, again, are we expanding in Europe?"

"You asked us the same question when we opened in L.A.," I said.

"Past luck is no guarantee for future luck," said Gunter. "What measures are you taking?"

Federico looked at me. "Should I..."

I hesitated.

"What measures are you taking to stop the losses?" repeated Gunter.

As I nodded, Federico left the conference room. We heard the echo of his disappearing footsteps from the high ceilings, then a sound of squeaking plastic wheels slowly came back to us. The sixteen-year-old painter reentered the room pushing a trolley, which displayed all the works: a pair of scissors, pink sea salt, matches, a bottle of water, and his famous oil. Federico positioned the trolley next to Gunny and poured some water in a pot and then dropped two spoons of oil.

"Hey, what's going on?" asked Gunter.

The painter looked inside the pot and nodded. "Yes, the oil is not floating up."

"What?" said Gunter, touching his well-combed ash-blond hair, growing increasingly agitated.

"What's going on, guys?" asked the chairman of Morgan Four Stones on the large videoconference screen.

"You asked which measures we took last time around, when things were slowing down," I said.

"Yes. What measures did you take?"

"We removed the bad luck."

"And allegedly Gunter, the representative of the Swiss Banks, brings bad luck?"

"Correct."

"*Nein. Nein,*" repeated Gunter compulsively.

The chairman cleared his throat trying to calm him down. "We're backstopping the Swiss financing, Gunter, we're backstopping your loans. We're in this together, please, Gunny."

Federico was given the go-ahead to carry out the bad luck removal ritual. Gunter's hair was washed, his scalp was dressed with olive oil, and his blond sideburns and the rest of his head were shaved. All along he continued to scream as if he was being skinned alive. The U.S. banks then agreed to extend our credit facilities.

When the board meeting finally ended and I walked out of the conference room, I took in the clear December night. I was losing track of time. In the hall, outside the window, the moon was climbing up the Gianicolo Hill and it was so bright it seemed alive. By contrast, the thoughts in my head were blurred.

"What the hell am I supposed to sign now?" I asked.

"Nothing," said Chloé sweetly, standing in front of the open window.

She was wearing a pair of jeans and a tweed jacket, and her long black curls fell on her shoulders like a stream of lava, just as they did the first night I had met her. She slipped two train tickets in my hand.

"What's this?" I asked, looking at the tickets.

"Let's take a break tonight. You've been working nineteen hours a day…you look awful. Let's take a break and go and make love," she said, almost begging me.

She smiled the way Marinella did the night of the accident, the moment before she stepped inside the car. She had that same gentle, defenseless smile.

"I need to talk to you," I said.

Chloé had decided to take an indefinite leave from SL&B and come with me to Italy. She said she was going to help with the company. At the beginning I was okay about it, almost flattered; after looking at today's numbers I was scared. If just a month ago our bakeries were slowing down but still in the black, now they were all losing money.

The previous month we'd worked around the clock trying to come up with solutions. We wouldn't even stop for lunch and continued to review market reports at night walking on the sidewalks of the Lungo Tevere, next to the river. Why were people suddenly not eating focaccia? Why was it no longer cool to stroll down the street with a slice in your hand? Why were our bakeries not a meeting point for teenagers anymore? How could we stop the banks from short-selling our stock (a trading technique that drove the price down)? Why was the downturn happening so fast?

Some evenings we would brainstorm reverse mergers at El Paino, a little pizza place on Via del

Lavatore, before a pizza so thin that we then asked for a discount. The fall air was still mild and it was nice to eat outside, next to the tall heat lamps. We walked hand in hand through the squares of Rome—Piazza Navona, Piazza di Spagna—discussing how we could improve the numbers. It was like making love in the time of earnings before interest, taxes, depreciation, and amortization. Almost always we stopped to kiss in Piazza della Quercia, the Square of the Oak, below the large and forever-green oak tree. I felt the beat of her heart, the steady, beautiful beat of her heart.

Then we would go back to our B&B and try to make love. Because of the company's difficult financial situation, we minimized expenses and stayed at a moderately priced room behind the Pantheon. I wanted her so badly, yet some nights I couldn't even touch her, and I felt a sense of rage and impotence and loss. Then we would have a cold shower standing up in our small bathtub.

On other evenings we went out to the Appia Antica, a great road of the Roman Empire ten minutes outside the city. For a moment the smell of the grass in November, the funny shape of the maritime pine trees, the washed-out marbles forgotten here and there made us think that everything was going to be okay. We walked through the cold Catacombs or in the mausoleum of Cecilia Metella, and continued to discuss accounting principles, comparing GAAP (Generally

Accepted Accounting Principles) to IFRS (International Financial Reporting Standards)—which would decrease the business's debt by close to $800 million— or we fought over the future of the company or said a prayer for the Maestro, thanks to whom we had first met. Then we'd forget our problems and run to eat the best carbonara pasta in a tavern called Qui' Non si Muore Mai, which means "Here you never die."

It was ten o'clock in the evening when the train stopped in a station in the open countryside. With the excuse that I needed a break, Chloé had put us on the first train to Saturnia, a little town known for its thermal baths. The Roman night was mild and sly.

"I have to talk to you," I said again, but she had already gotten off and started walking along the tracks. I followed her. The station's lights receded behind us. Chloé held a map of the area as if she was looking for the treasure that could save the company. Then she took off her jeans in the December night and ran down a slope, and I followed her slender, naked legs and her Uniqlo white panties.

We entered a pine grove. The moon illuminated the water and the thermal bath was covered in fog. It glittered. After she tested the water with the tip of her bare toe, Chloé softly slid into the pond. She threw off her panties.

"Come here," she said, taking me inside of her.

And we made love for the last time. For the last time, I kissed her beautiful mouth, her small firm breasts, her singing nipples, her belly button that had more fire than a volcano, and every little inch of her skin. The yellow fumes rose in the cold air, and you could barely see the sky from the pine grove, and she tasted sweet and salty and a bit hardened, like a slice of leftover focaccia.

"See, you could build a bakery in all of the beautiful places in the world, like this one," she said, stretching her arms to the sky. "But the world wouldn't necessarily be a better place."

"I have got to talk to you, Chloé," I said, holding her hand.

"Why do you continue to open new bakeries and hire people?"

"I wanted to do something great and beautiful," I said. "I am trapped inside my own dream."

"You're trapped inside the banks' dream."

I looked at her, hoping that what I was about to tell her would make things easier, would make my breaking up with her something she'd want.

"Chloé, there are forty dollars of debt per dollar of equity," I said. "You'd better run, or this is going to drag you down."

"So what?" she said calmly. "Why don't we go to New York and try to put things back together?"

When we returned to our B&B it was two o'clock in the morning. Winter had suddenly arrived also in the Eternal City, the mild Roman night had turned evil, and the air was cold and crystalline. Even the marble sculptures of the Bernini in Piazza Navona seemed to shiver. I diligently folded my shirts inside my bag, concentrating on each single movement, trying not to think about the rest, because if I did, I wouldn't be able to do it.

"Where are you going?" she asked.

I walked through the corridor to the elevator.

"Are we returning to New York to put things back together?" she said again, with a ray of hope.

Again she looked at me, defenseless, like Marinella the night of the accident, the moment before she stepped inside the car. Then, all of a sudden, she understood, and two silent tears ran down her cheeks.

"You don't think I can help you?" she asked. She held my hand and smiled. "Are you firing me?"

I felt the weight of her fingers inside the palm of my hand. Now her smile and her tears created some sort of rainbow on her cheek.

"Are you breaking up with me, Rosso?"

I went to look for my voice, for some word, inside my throat, but I couldn't find anything, so I left.

I had failed at the only thing that really mattered to me: not to hurt her. The Christ of the Abyss had not granted my greatest prayer. I had managed to ruin the person who wasn't afraid to jump into a tiger's cage, a girl filled with desires who deserved a career, a beautiful family, and a future, and not to face an endless trial and then spend the rest of her days in jail.

CHLOÉ VERDI

m s. Verdi is right, she hadn't managed to help him," the prosecutor said in the most hurtful way, looking at me. "Defendant Rosso Fiorentino had not changed. He was the same careless party boy who had simply gone from his grandfather's tuxedo jacket to a double-breasted suit. He was neither capable of spending money nor of counting it. Everything continued to slip through his hands like the steering wheel on the night of the car accident seven years before."

A prosecutor's job is to point fingers. The truth is always more complicated. A start-up company is like a child: sometimes it has a growth spurt, sometimes it throws tantrums, and sometimes it gets sick. In this case all the mishaps came at once: the banks (for their own interests) had continued to throw money at the company as if there was no tomorrow; and the other banks who were not involved were betting against it and dragging the price down; instead of repaying some of its debt, the company continued to expand beyond the market's capacity (as Martin, the bum-economist, warned); Don Otto had left and the focaccia's quality had dropped to a moccasin's sole; and Rosso, instead of cutting jobs and restructuring, continued to manage Focaccia House as if it were a not-for-profit by feeding bums for free, refusing to fire people, and sending profits to the Christ of the Abyss (believing that he had to honor his vow to a local Ligurian patron just like a $2.2 billion credit facility with JP Morgan). Any of these factors alone would have resulted in a mild cold for what had been a healthy company; all together they caused its collapse. And there was no time to react: once again everything had happened overnight, like a stroke that takes down the strongest body in just a few minutes.

Leonard Sterlicht, the public attorney, swiftly approached the bench to deliver his final arguments. Although he was in his mid-fifties he seemed in good form, not an ounce of extra fat under his cobalt-blue suit. He had a clear complexion, thick, curly white hair, and soft long lips. His entire persona made you feel comfortable, almost at ease. Yet, if you looked at him carefully, his eyes had no expression. Like a moray that's about to strike.

"Now we know the defendant's story," he began. "This jury knows the rest. On December 20, 2,502 bakeries reported losses of approximately $82.1 billion. On January 2, Focaccia House defaulted on its 172 financing facilities. On January 5, the six leading banks that had financed the company collapsed, followed the day after by the collapse of Fortitude Retirement Fund, the fund that had purchased Focaccia House's securities. On January 11, FIG Insurance Company was indicted for rating the fund's securities as Triple-A."

The prosecutor faced the jury.

"On January 17, Focaccia House filed for Chapter 11, entered into bankruptcy, and was indicted by the SEC on nineteen counts, including negligence and fraud. Concerning the count of fraud, this prosecution is seeking 137 years of imprisonment for defendant Rosso Fiorentino. This is the maximum sentence provided by law, but minimal if compared to the consequences of the defendant's actions and the damages he caused. Damages to you, the jury."

The public prosecutor paused and rubbed his heart-shaped mouth, which said the nastiest things in the kindest possible way.

"The downturn has thus no longer affected only the banks. Insurance companies that believed in a 'nonmeat diet' and invested their assets in Focaccia House are facing hard times. Tech companies that put their money on what they thought to be a real product have lost their savings. Automakers that diversified their portfolio when FH was trading at a multiple of a 102 times earnings are struggling. The downturn has trickled down to the real economy, the real world, and real people, to you the jury and your families. On January 19, in one session, the Dow Jones dropped 666 points."

· JOB 18 ·

The Verdict

CHLOÉ VERDI

May 16, 2009, New York City

When on Tuesday, May 11, 2009, I entered the courtroom, I immediately noticed that Federal Justice Henrietta Pontia Pilgrims was wearing the same Bleu de France suit, the same coral necklace as the day before; combined with those circles under her eyes I concluded that she had pulled an all-nighter to decide what she was about to say.

She nodded to the prosecution, Leonard Sterlicht, and then to the defense attorney, Jay Clark, although she found him to be terribly irritating. Jay Clark was a rosy-cheeked idealist, a twenty-six-year-old fresh out of law school, a totally unknown entity in the court system. All of the major firms had, in fact, declined to take on the case and represent Rosso Fiorentino. Not only had Clark not entered a single guilty plea on behalf of the defendant, which would have made the case much simpler, he had also taken the unprecedented position that Rosso Fiorentino was not guilty on any count, not even negligence. From the prospective of the need to find a culprit, the most annoying thing about Jay Clark was that he was talented and obsessively zealous: each of his statements was followed by a quote from at least one case law including the circuit and the page number. Beneath his rosy cheeks and passionate gray eyes, he seemed to hide the twelve-CD Westlaw encyclopedia.

"Let us hear the summations," said Judge Pilgrims. "The jury may then retire to the jury room to begin deliberating."

I could tell that most of the jurors had made up their minds, which, for some reason, I did not consider a good sign. Even the redheaded New Rochelle housewife, with whom I had bonded visually throughout my testimony, no longer gave me a hopeful smile.

"The prosecution may begin," said the Judge.

The prosecutor, Leonard Sterlicht, stood up, his curly white hair shining, his motionless moray eyes awakened by instinct. "The facts are on the record," he began, setting aside his well-reviewed notes. "As to motives, this jury may believe the defense: that the defendant wanted to feed the world, wanted to do something 'great and beautiful,' that he paid in cash 750,000 dollars to a homeless man for his 'financial services,' that COA stands for Christ of the Abyss, and that the defendant wired more than 2.6 billion dollars to an account in the name of a statue while the company was collapsing." The prosecutor paused. "Even if the jury believes this fairy tale, the case is proven *in re ipsa*. The key distinction between fraud and negligence is that, in the case of negligence, one does not know what one is doing. Here, the defendant knew perfectly well what he was doing. He was advised all along by Wall Street's number one law firm, thanks to Ms. Verdi.

"Ladies and gentlemen of the jury, this is not a love story. There is nothing romantic about any of this. Ms. Verdi perfectly knew that Rosso Fiorentino was incapable of running a business, that he was a good-for-nothing, that he couldn't even keep a dog on a leash, and yet, with her glossy, well-prepared filings and cute smile, she duped the SEC into approving the IPO, and the banks into loaning billions, and investors into investing trillions. Ms. Verdi needed Rosso to advance her career as a lawyer: remember, before the IPO, she was reorganizing law books in the library. And Rosso needed her: what other blue-chip firm, or law firm in general, would have assisted this wacko, financed by pornographers and advised by bums? Who, if not Ms. Verdi, could and did 'save' Focaccia House's IPO?" The prosecutor paused. He knew what would be the deciding factor in the jury's mind and went for it mercilessly. "Ladies and gentlemen of the jury, this is not a love story but a Ponzi scheme. They knew it and you, the people, know it too."

As I heard those last words, I felt a cold shiver down my spine. He is guilty, and I am too. The prosecution will press charges against me.

"The defense may proceed," the Judge said.

I held my breath, looking up desperately at the defense, at the twenty-six-year-old Jay Clark. Deliver the most amazing argument, come up with something.

But instead he had a one-liner.

"Rosso Fiorentino is not guilty," said Jay Clark, and sat down again.

The Judge put on her white-framed glasses, frowning.

"The defense does not wish to make a final statement? You claim that defendant is not guilty on any count, not even negligence?"

Jay Clark stood up again. His gray eyes sparkled immensely this time.

"The defendant created two million jobs. Five different consulting firms—three of which were appointed by this prosecution—undertake that half of those jobs can be saved with a restructuring. Would anyone in this courtroom object if I said that I could create one million jobs? If I said that my financial consultant was homeless, and that for each dollar I made I paid one dollar to Buddha, Moses, Shiva, or the Christ of the Abyss? Would anybody object if I created one million jobs?"

The courtroom stood silent. Even the prosecutor caressed his cheek as if he had been whacked in the face.

"We have to be careful about blaming the defendant for our own faults," continued Jay Clark. "No matter how large Focaccia House's market capitalization may be, it would be ridiculous to hold it responsible for the financial meltdown, as the prosecution seems to be doing. It would be like blaming a squirrel for an earthquake. It's like saying that by robbing a hot dog stand in Singapore one can cause the collapse of Wall Street. And if that is the case, if the laws of cause and effect of our hyperconnected world have indeed become so fragile and incomprehensible, then responsibilities ought to be sought elsewhere.

"Case law is well established. Negligence is to be evaluated based on our society's moral standards. Did the defendant fail to behave with the level of care that an ordinary prudent man would have exercised under the same circumstances?

"There is no doubt that Rosso Fiorentino made mistakes, that he took on risks, that in hindsight he should have consolidated the company's growth and not continued to expand it endlessly, but he did not deviate from today's moral standards. America's 'ordinary, prudent man' is encouraged, indeed forced, to take extraordinary risks in order to survive. Are the millions of people who buy their homes with a 20 percent down payment and an 80 percent loan negligent? If so every family, every businessman, every bank, every person in this courtroom, is guilty of negligence. And are we accusing a woman for loving her man and standing by him in failure? How can Americans be encouraged to succeed, if we, the people, shoot the losers?"

As the defense concluded its argument, I felt a sparkle of hope. He's innocent! He's innocent! I shook my head smiling. It made no sense. One moment I thought he was guilty, the next that he was innocent.

"The jury may retire to the jury room to begin deliberating," said Judge Pilgrims.

The jurors stood up. I looked at each of them. Their faces too seemed to have a sparkle of warmth, as if that last speech had made their desires possible, or at least imaginable; even the redheaded New Rochelle housewife seemed to think the closing arguments protected her. Or maybe not. Maybe they had already made up their minds, and their faint smiles were simply due to the idea of being done with it.

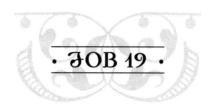

· JOB 19 ·

Something Great
and Beautiful

CHLOÉ VERDI

May 26, 2009, New York City

Remember," I said, showing the palms of my hands to the bakers sitting in the conference room. "Nobody can use them the way you do."

While a photo of Rapallo faded on the screen, I passed out the materials to the aspiring bakers seated in the conference room of the company's new office on Astoria Boulevard, Queens. I was wearing the white-and-blue-striped T-shirt I wore at the seaside in Italy, which exposed my navel, although my hips felt bigger and rounder.

"And Don Otto will talk to you about preparation and baking," I said, winking at him as he walked in.

I left the conference room and climbed up the stairs two at a time. Our new company headquarters did not have an elevator. We were now located in an inexpensive warehouse in Queens, close to where the first bakery had opened. When I reached the top floor I felt dizzy for a moment. I pressed my index finger against the bridge of my nose and took a deep breath to regain my balance. I shouldn't have been surprised, I thought, as I caught a glimpse of the corporate-looking succulent plant on my desk. I knew that one day I'd become the CEO of something. I paced my steps on the gray executive rug of the long corridor. Instead of charging me with conspiracy, the court had appointed me as the company's interim CEO. Everything had happened overnight, as is sometimes the case when judges have to deal with a case they don't like. I had another dizzy spell. I was nauseated again. I leaned against the corridor's railing and took a deeper breath. Why did you have to go? I reached out to my twin scar. Don't you want me to put this baby of yours into the world? I walked to Sachin's office at the end of the corridor. The door was half open.

"You're late. Are you going to be finished before you take off tonight?" I asked.

"Yes. The results only just came in from Palo Alto," Sachin said, apologizing. In reality, he was still going over the balance sheet's data line by line, knowing that, with just one glance, I would spot anything that was off.

"Are you doing accounting or creative writing?" I asked, smiling. I had noticed that, with his elbow, Sachin had pushed Focaccia House's balance sheet over his writing notebook.

"Creative accounting," he said. His voice was tired and a bit happy. He already knew that a good day of writing is always followed by a sleepless night because one is so wired. "Okay, I started writing again," he admitted. "I'm also searching for the Venus again." Then he swiveled in his chair and looked at me. With his eyes he touched my stomach. "Are you coming with us? Are you going to tell him?"

I rested my hands on my hips, which were slowly losing their shape, and I felt an irrepressible smile.

"I can no longer fly. I have a doctor's appointment today. Will you tell him?"

"No," said Sachin. "You should tell him. I think he'll come back if you tell him."

ROSSO FIORENTINO

June 2, 2009, West Bengal, India

I looked at the thick binders where my past and future were neatly organized. The Indian night was humid. The silence was almost complete. I could only hear the whistle of the wind against the monastery's stone wall. Since the trial ended and I left New York I'd repeated the decision to myself every so often. After I did, I would feel better for some time, then my head would start spinning, and I would feel sick, as if I'd had too much to drink.

"On the first count, breach of duty of care, this jury finds defendant Rosso Fiorentino...*guilty.*

"On the second count, negligence, this jury finds defendant Rosso Fiorentino...*guilty.*

"On the nineteen counts of breach of the duty of loyalty and fraud, this jury finds defendant Rosso Fiorentino...*not guilty.*

"The request for imprisonment is denied."

I stood in the monastery cell, my forehead drenched. I felt a sense of temporary relief, as if

I had just vomited. My apartment and all of my belongings were sold at auction. Some $2.6 billion were repatriated from the Christ of the Abyss, and the bankruptcy trustee was able to recover enough assets to restore people's retirement savings. I wasn't behind bars, but I never knew whether or not to feel relieved.

The edges of the sky began to turn gray. There was the cry of an animal that measured the distance outside, the distance among the prairies, the mountains, the ocean, the city, the buzzing sound of life, and there, where I was. The bell tolled the dawn prayer. I felt my knees buckling. I fell to the ground and joined my hands in prayer. I was alone and afraid. I prayed about the car accident and about this new accident. Despite all of my best intentions, my life was a series of accidents. And nobody listened, not even the Christ of the Abyss (maybe because his payment was revoked).

"I only fuck up down here. Can I come up with you?"

As my hands were joined at my mouth, I felt a presence in the room. The air was filled with a strong, sweet smell. Instead of the Christ of the Abyss, a white-and-yellow-pinstriped jacket, a coat of gel, and two tanned cheeks appeared before my eyes.

"You did what I couldn't do...," said a voice I thought I recognized. Then a deep laughter followed.

"You've done something great and beautiful. Don't be such a crybaby!" I had? And what was that?

When I first heard the sound of the engine, it was probably an hour after dawn. My eyes were closed. I heard the sound from afar, climbing the mountains at first, and then approaching on the dusty road. When the car stopped in front of the monastery, the silence was almost complete again.

There was a loud roar (the two-thousand-year-old door opens) followed by footsteps. The footsteps echoed in the long corridor, bouncing off the thick walls, coming toward my cell. According to the monastery's rules, visitors could only come in one at a time. My friends each brought me a gift as if it was my birthday.

"It's on the house," Don Otto said. He smiled and handed me a baked pan of focaccia.

Sachin, who came in second, offered as his gift all the latest gossip: that Don Otto was back, that the company was doing better, that Chloé was the new CEO, that the Dow Jones was picking up two hundred points a week, that Verger had kept his promise and given up porn, and that Buvlovski was disbarred for life for failing to supervise the case and had moved to Tajikistan to work as a paralegal in Juncal's law firm.

"And I've started writing again!" he said, almost blushing.

Then his face gradually changed expression, from excitement to concern. He now no longer had that tic causing him to look up as if something were about to crash on him, because everything already had. He pointed to the frail young man kneeling in the small cell in front of mine. "You're not going to take vows, right? You won't have to give up focaccia?"

In the cell opposite mine, a young novice with long black eyelashes was kneeling on a blanket. He had taken the vow of silence. He could not speak, could not eat meat, cheese, flour, or eggs, and could wash himself only at two o'clock in the morning. The first year he could still receive letters and read them but could no longer respond. The second year he couldn't even open them.

"Promise you won't take vows?" asked Sachin.

I was hoping that the greatest gossiper of all time would tell me more, would tell me about the only thing I cared to hear of, would help me decipher the Maestro's words and give me a reason to stick around, but he didn't.

Around seven, after the bell finished tolling the second prayer of the morning, the door of my cell creaked again.

"How did the two of you get in?" I asked.

Without responding, Federico and Franz sat on the ground and unwrapped the tray that Don Otto had brought for me. They shared the focaccia with their oil-stained fingers. Then they told me that they had to wait, that the monk in charge wouldn't let more people in, and that he was tougher than all of New York City's bouncers put together and couldn't care less if they had come with Sachin and Don Otto all the way from the United States.

"C'mon, have a slice," said the painter, handing me a piece of focaccia.

"C'mon, have some, don't be such a downer!" Franz said. "Success doesn't exist without failure. You've still given jobs to a million people."

I hesitated, thinking again about the vision I had this morning. I'm sure it was the Maestro. I heard his words again.

"Is it true that Chloé is pregnant?" I asked.

Federico wrapped up the empty tray and put it away.

It was already daytime. The first morning noises came from the monastery's walls.

People do many things to find a meaning in life. Some, like the Maestro, understand everything when their life is over in India; some work eighteen hours a day, like Dimitri Buvlovski; some, like me, run after petroleum-green eyes. Some defend and prosecute the fine line between success and failure.

There are people who don't need to find a meaning in life, because they haven't lived yet, because their best years were taken from them. Chloé wasn't interested in finding a meaning. She was all about living. For her it was all about getting into the University of Chicago, finding a job, falling in love, helping Shimoto, saving my dream.

Then there are people like Franz, the better ones, who keep on partying until morning comes.

"Is it true?" I asked Franz again, waiting for that one and only answer. "Is she pregnant?"

Franz placed his face in the palms of my hands, just as when he visited me at the hospital after the car crash, when Marinella had died.

But this time he didn't cry. He smiled.

ACKNOWLEDGMENTS

This book has taken so much time and generosity from all of my friends that the thank-you list could be as long as the book itself. And these words can express only a small part of my gratitude.

First of all, I wish to thank my publisher, Judith Gurewich, for her endless dedication and encouragement, and the very long hours and months she spent working on this story, and to all of the wonderful team at Other Press for making it possible.

Thank you to my wife, Katrina, and to my children Margherita, Sofia, and Maximus for being here. And to Kelly and Dean.

Thank you to Emmanuelle de Villepin for our literary friendship and for introducing me to Judith, and to my agent, Susan Golomb, and to Cindy Spiegel with gratitude. And to Chris Pereira and Clayton Harley. And of course to Donald Bogle for his club movie nights that remain as much a ritual as Sunday Mass.

Thank you to Kip Williams, Gretchen Mol, and Tod Harrison Williams for their friendship that is as long as my time in New York, and to Tod Williams and Billie

Tsien, and of course to David Tisch, and Anne Carey, and to all my colleagues at Pellegrini & Mendoza, to my friends and colleagues Luis Mendoza and Pato De Groote, Kenneth Regensburg, and Jack Heinberg, to Judith White and Michael Yi for the long hours and great results, to Phil Power and to Marjorie Sanon.

Thank you to Ram Sundaram and his wife, Preethi Krishna, for the loving fun and for allowing me to write these pages in the midst of their fabulous summer dinner parties in the Hamptons.

Thank you to Vanessa von Bismarck and her husband, Max Weiner, for their long-lasting friendship throughout these years. And to Dennis Paul and Coralie Charriol. And of course to Marianna Kulukundis. Thank you to Joerg, Imssy, and Kristina Klebe for having first welcomed me on 62nd Street, and the Deseglise family.

Thank you to my schoolmate Ferdinand Calice and his wife, Teresa, for the time in Chicago, Portofino, and New York, and for allowing me to use Ferdinand's name in this book without lawsuits. Thank you to Marie and Tino Liechtenstein for our Hamptons adventures, and to Philippe Metternich.

Thank you to Bob Roth and Reza Ali for introducing me to Transcendental Meditation, which has changed my life.

Thank you to my cousins Giulia Marletta, Alexandra Pappas, and Louis Tsiros for their affection, and newborn Sonny Winthrop. And of course Zia Maria Sapounakis, and to Amanda Ross and how inspiring she has been to the children, to Ali Iz for a work relationship that turned into friendship, and thank you to Antonio Monda for writing the most perceptive interview of my father's work and to his wife Jacquie's hospitality.

Thank you to Iliane and Anthony Ogilvie Thompson, although geographically far away always present, and always generous with their minds and souls. And thank you to Michelle Clark for opening her home on many Thanksgivings.

Thank you to Charles Bischoff, Carolyn, Oliver, Max, and my goddaughter Carina, and Lady Bischoff and Sir Win; many pages of this book were written under the roofs of their nurturing homes in England and Tuscany. And of course to Kinvara Balfour, Sam Elworthy, Will Nevin, Patty Sinclair, and George and Lizzie Lewis, and a super mega thank-you to Maxine Sloss. Thank you to Abby Weisman for inspiring the friendship among our children. And to Annie Borello and her beautiful pictures.

Thank you to all the members of the Sicilian Expedition: Jim and Elise McVeigh, Alan and Jacqueline Mitchell, Ana and Peter von Schlossberg, Lauren Peters, Kat Cohen, Lorenzo Lorenzotti, Vinod Krishnan, and of course to my dear Raghu Sundaram, Pialy and Nakul Krishnaswamy, and Nikkel Krishnaswamy.

Thank you to all the wonderful amazing evenings with Chiara and Jamie Mai, Dayssi and Paul Kanavos, Catrine and Chris Salz. And a special big thank-you to Wright and Valerie Colas-Orhstrom, Clemence and William von Mueffling, and to Andrew and Barbara Gundlach, Enrica and Fabrizio Arrigo Bentivoglio, Monica Fuentes and Alberto Recchi, Imogen Lloyd Weber, and thank you to Lucy Sikes and her husband, Euan Rallie, to Ed Epstein and his summer terrace, and Meredith Ostrom, Ghislain and Elena de Noüe, and my great neighbors Olivia and Christophe Maubert, and of course to Italy's biggest fan, Neil Sidi.

Thank you to Anthony Todd, Alvin Valley, and Nevil Dwek, and their ability to turn things into art, to Nicolò Vergani for pointing me to the moon, and Fabrizio Volterra for many good chats, and Michael and Cheyne Beys. A very special thank-you to Meg Sharpe for helping so much with my father's art.

Thank you to Giorgio van Straten for our conversations about literature, and to Ennio Ranaboldo and his inspiring quotes, and Annie Churchill and Nick and all the good dinners, Anne Marie and Irik Sevin for the wonderful time in the Hamptons. Thank you to Lloyd Nathan and his wife, Elana, for always being good friends.

Thank you to Max Hoover and Tatiana Boncompagni and the time at the Farm, in the wonderful company of Philipp and Christa Carr swimming in creeks, thank you to Jim and Jacques-Henry Cointreau for the most powerful writing, Georgina Rylance and Peppe Ciardi and discovering Porto Ercole, and of course to Richard David Story and Jennifer, and Steve De Luca, and to John Josephson and Carolina Zapf. Thank you to Daria Colombo and Tobias for our cross-generational lifelong friendship.

Thank you to Richard Armstrong, Marco Leona, and Ian Alteveer for many conversations about the arts. And to Jacques Derrida for reciting the verses of Corneille's *Le Cid*.

Thank you to Daisy Prince and her husband, Hugh Chisholm, for their Spring Fling and time in Newport, Chiara Clemente and Tyler for our creative ventures, to Charlotte Clark and Johnny and Poppy and our cross-border friendship, Veronica and Anna Bulgari and the time in Millbrook, and to Damian Fraser for being such a great friend, and of course to his mother, the exceptional writer Antonia Fraser, to Lucy and Annamaria Fato, James and Ellen Berkley, Nicholas Barclay, Ron Weinberg and his wife, Terri, when they come to New York, Sam and Danielle Lipton, to Colin Harley and our motorbike rides, and Anita Laudone and her wonderful paintings.

Thank you to all our REDS family: Sarah Messmore, Rhea Shome, and Sharon Lickerman for being so meaningful in Maximus' young life, and to Greg Tolaram and Molly for her patience and delicious coffee, and Raj. And to all our friends at REDS: Simon and Kara Gerson, Dennis and Roseline Neveling, and Casey and David Moore and our Greek Nights, to Theodore Harris and Deborah, Donald and Juliana Rosenfeld and our art adventures, Giacomo and Kate Picco, Jeffrey and Elizabeth Leeds, thank you to Claudia and Bartle Bull, Michael and Nina Patterson, Esmeralda Spinola and her husband, Emilio, and of course Gaya and Vinay Nair for endless adventures. And thank you to Arianna and Chris Martell for a wonderful Fourth of July.

And thank you for the time in California especially to Jim and Bill Deutch, Hanako Williams, and Matt Feinstein.

Thank you to our departed, but always present, Federico Fellini and Giulietta Masina for guiding me in Rome. Thank you to Gaston Salvatore and to Joseph Brodsky for the time in Venice and for inspiring a central character of this book. Thank you to Jonathan Franzen for allowing me to share with him a restored copy of *The Leopard* by Luchino Visconti, and to Umberto Eco for teaching me that to become a writer in a way is like entertaining a career in the military.

And thank you to the bakery Le Pellegrine in the Italian Riviera whose extraordinary focaccia has indeed inspired much of my childhood and this book.